BROBOTS™

AND THE SHOUJO SHENANIGANS!

ONI PRESS

ONI
PRESS
PRESENTS

BRO

AND THE

EDITED BY
ROBIN HERRERA

BOTS™

SHOUJO SHENANIGANS!

WRITTEN BY
J. TORRES

ART, LETTERING,
& DESIGN BY
SEAN DOVE

PUBLISHED BY ONI PRESS, INC.

JOE NOZEMACK, FOUNDER & CHIEF FINANCIAL OFFICER
JAMES LUCAS JONES, PUBLISHER
CHARLIE CHU, V.P. OF CREATIVE & BUSINESS DEVELOPMENT
BRAD ROOKS, DIRECTOR OF OPERATIONS
MELISSA MESZAROS, DIRECTOR OF PUBLICITY
MARGOT WOOD, DIRECTOR OF SALES
RACHEL REED, MARKETING MANAGER
AMBER O'NEILL, SPECIAL PROJECTS MANAGER
TROY LOOK, DIRECTOR OF DESIGN & PRODUCTION
HILARY THOMPSON, SENIOR GRAPHIC DESIGNER
KATE Z. STONE, JUNIOR GRAPHIC DESIGNER
SONJA SYNAK, JUNIOR GRAPHIC DESIGNER
ANGIE KNOWLES, DIGITAL PREPRESS LEAD
ARI YARWOOD, EXECUTIVE EDITOR
ROBIN HERRERA, SENIOR EDITOR
DESIREE WILSON, ASSOCIATE EDITOR
ALISSA SALLAH, ADMINISTRATIVE ASSISTANT
JUNG LEE, LOGISTICS ASSOCIATE
SCOTT SHARKEY, WAREHOUSE ASSISTANT

ONIPRESS.COM

FACEBOOK.COM/ONIPRESS
TWITTER.COM/ONIPRESS
ONIPRESS.TUMBLR.COM
INSTAGRAM.COM/ONIPRESS

Find J. TORRES online at

JTORRESCOMICS.COM
@JTORRESCOMICS

Find SEAN DOVE online at

ANDTHANKYOUFORFLYING.COM
@ANDTHANKYOU

FIRST EDITION: AUGUST 2018

ISBN 978-1-62010-521-4
eISBN 978-1-62010-522-1

PRINTED IN CHINA

LIBRARY OF CONGRESS CONTROL NUMBER: 2017961743

1 2 3 4 5 6 7 8 9 10

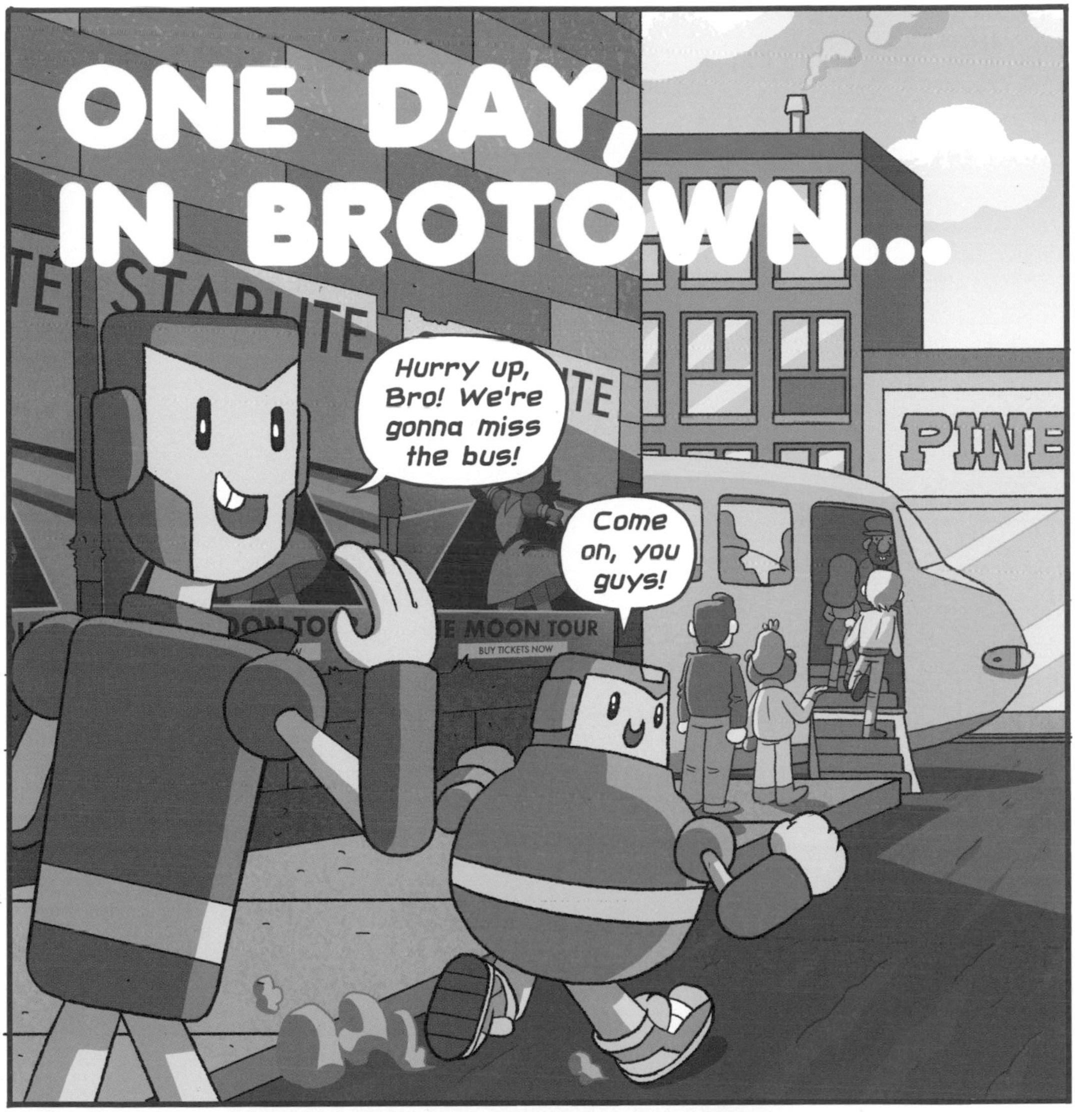
ONE DAY, IN BROTOWN...
STARLITE
Hurry up, Bro! We're gonna miss the bus!
Come on, you guys!
MOON TOUR
BUY TICKETS NOW
PINE

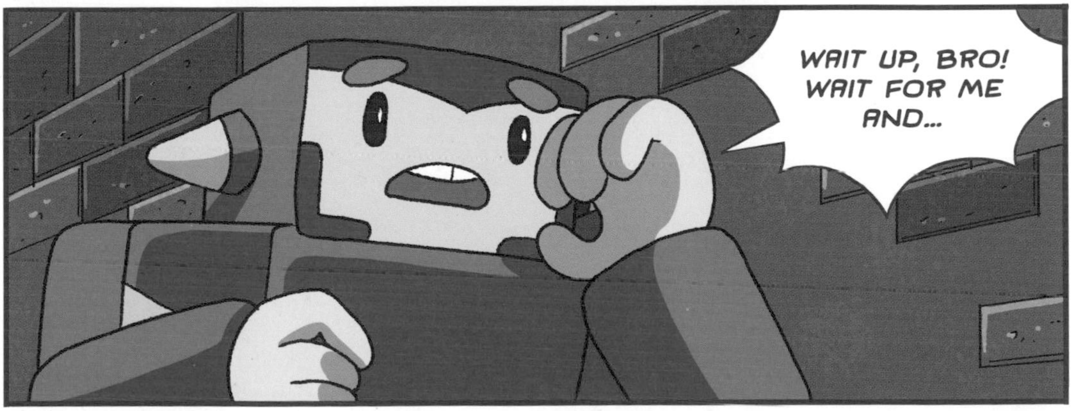
WAIT UP, BRO! WAIT FOR ME AND...

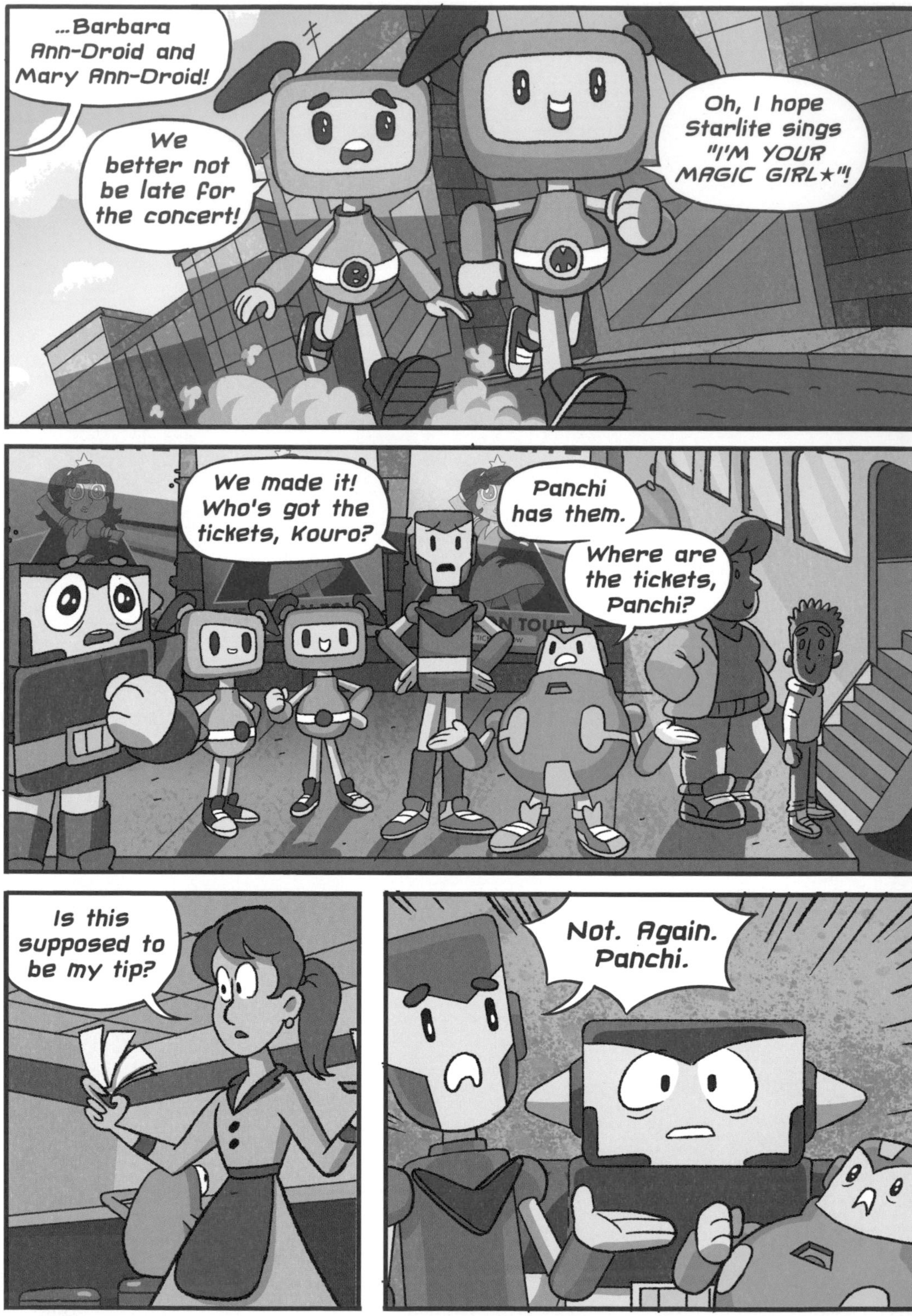
...Barbara Ann-Droid and Mary Ann-Droid!
We better not be late for the concert!
Oh, I hope Starlite sings "I'M YOUR MAGIC GIRL★"!
We made it! Who's got the tickets, Kouro?
Panchi has them.
Where are the tickets, Panchi?
Is this supposed to be my tip?
Not. Again. Panchi.

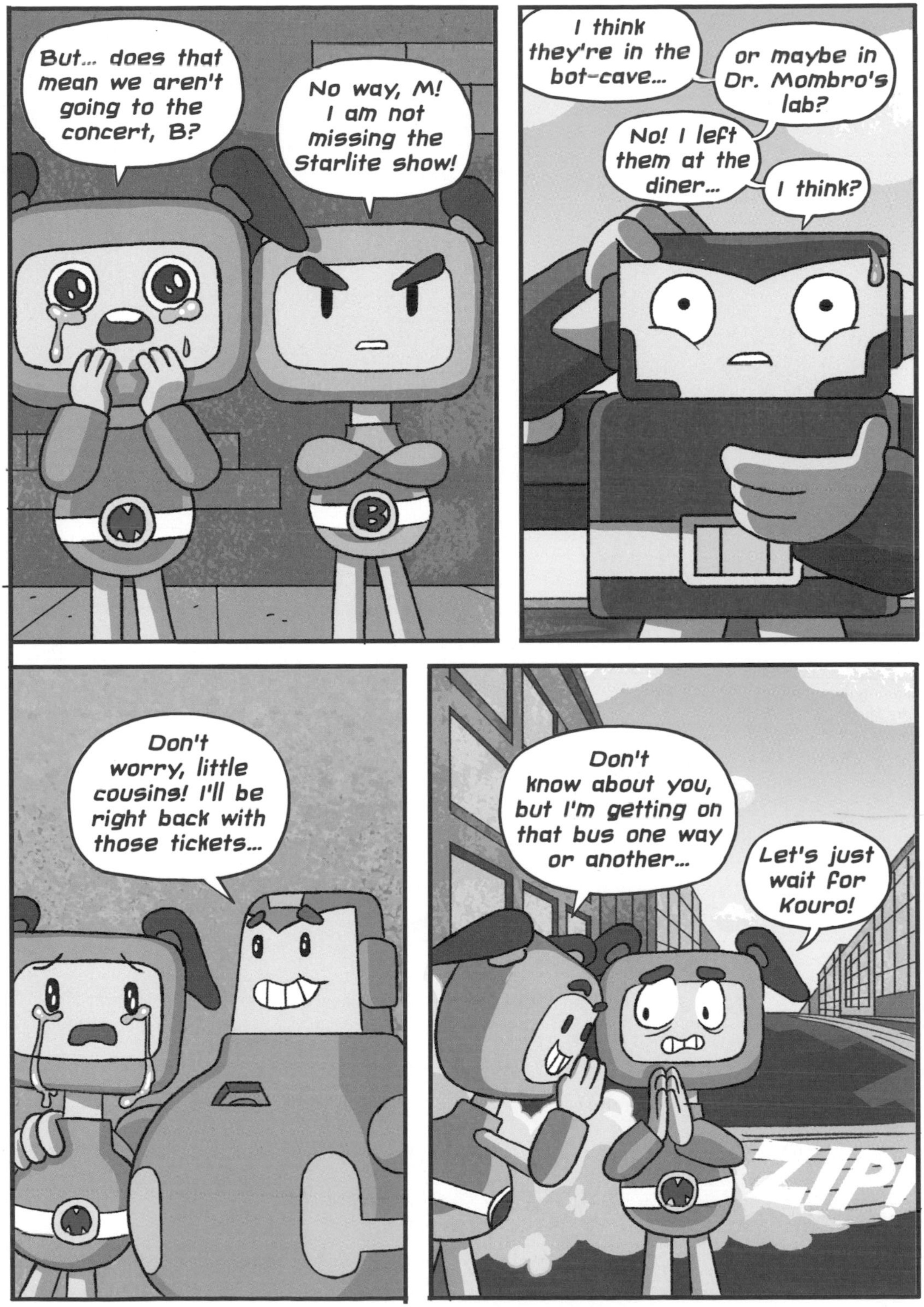
But... does that mean we aren't going to the concert, B?
No way, M! I am not missing the Starlite show!
I think they're in the bot-cave...
or maybe in Dr. Mombro's lab?
No! I left them at the diner...
I think?
Don't worry, little cousins! I'll be right back with those tickets...
Don't know about you, but I'm getting on that bus one way or another...
Let's just wait for Kouro!
ZIP!

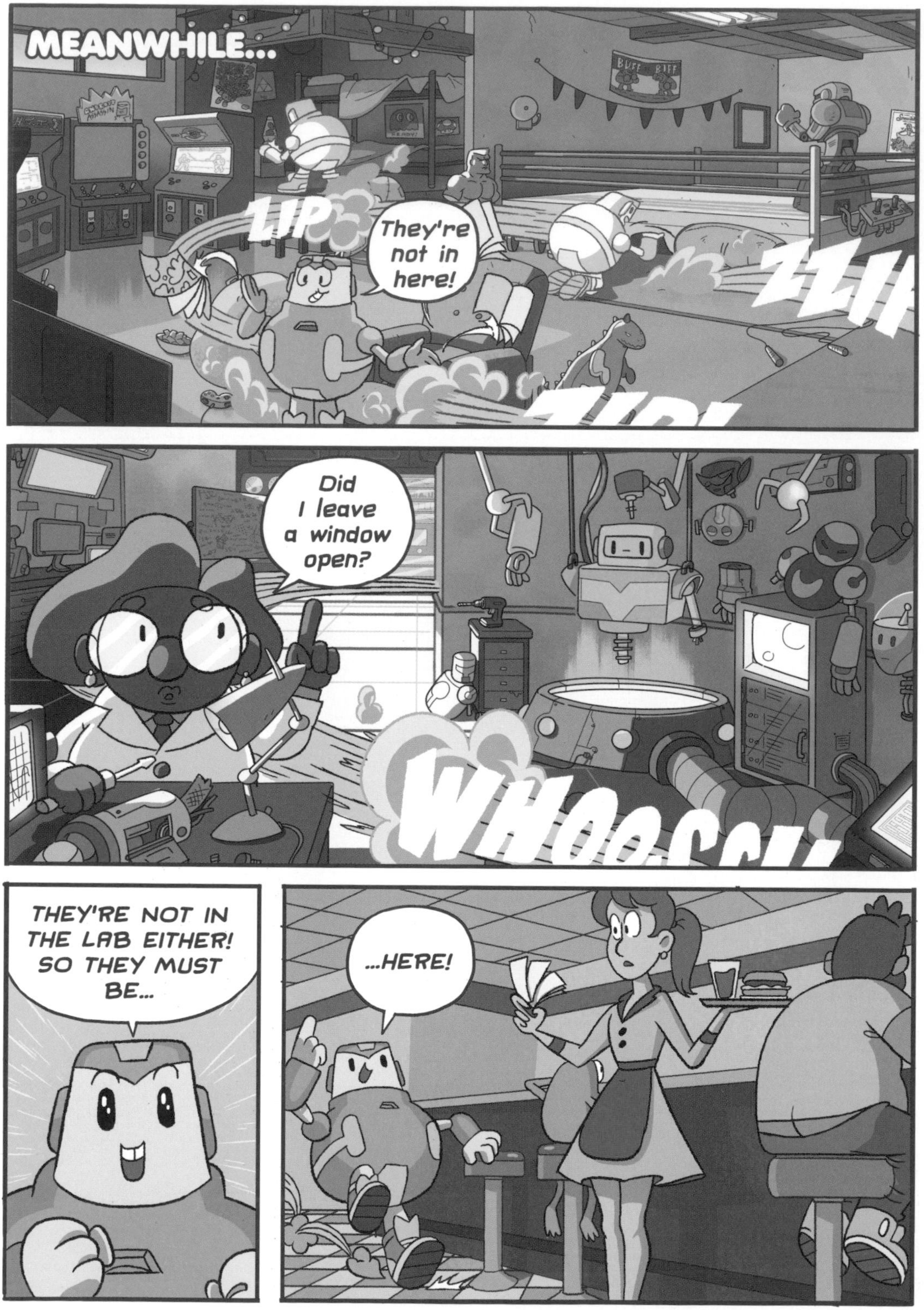
MEANWHILE...
ZIP
They're not in here!
Did I leave a window open?
THEY'RE NOT IN THE LAB EITHER! SO THEY MUST BE...
...HERE!

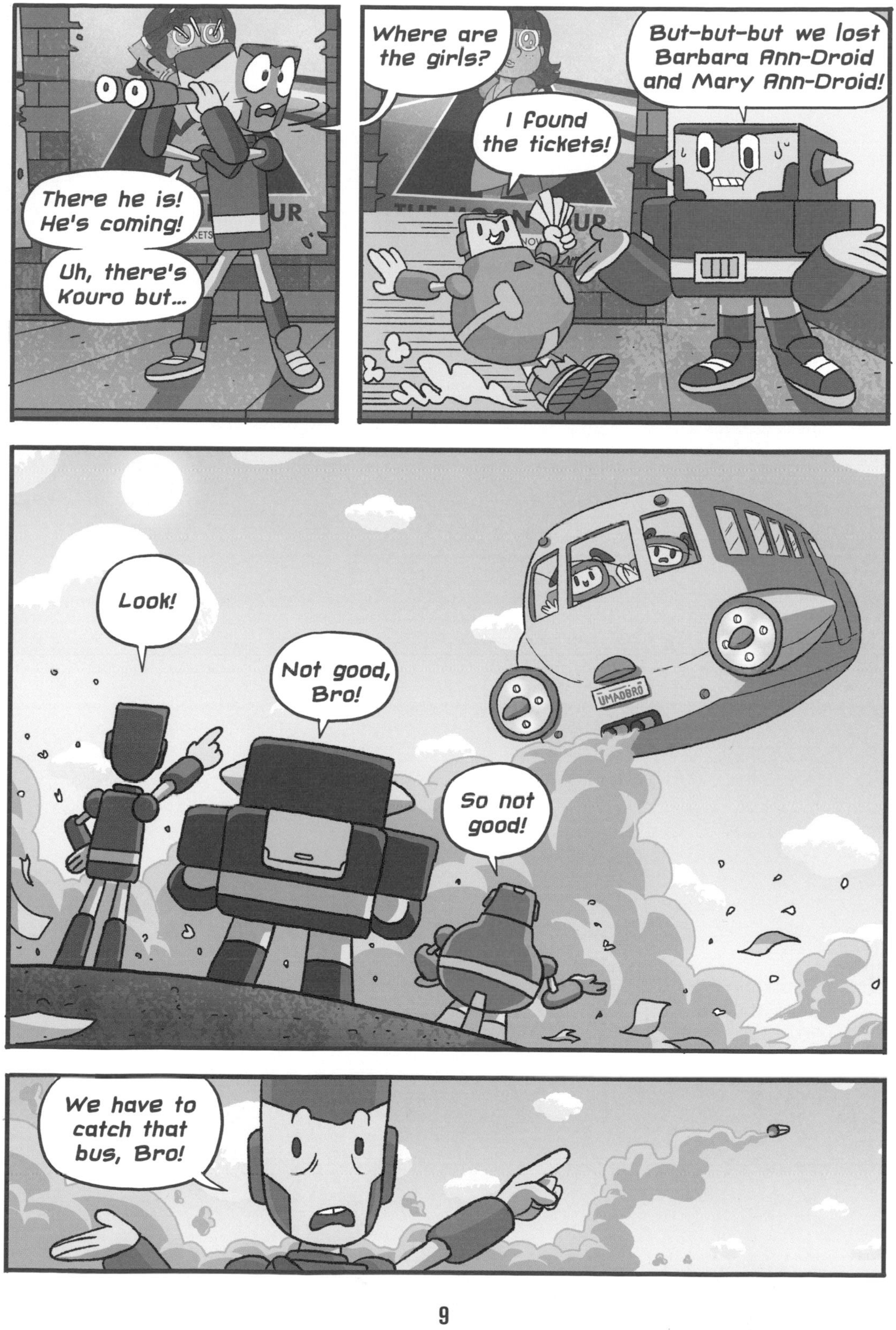
There he is! He's coming!
Uh, there's Kouro but...
Where are the girls?
I found the tickets!
But-but-but we lost Barbara Ann-Droid and Mary Ann-Droid!
Look!
Not good, Bro!
UMADBRO
So not good!
We have to catch that bus, Bro!

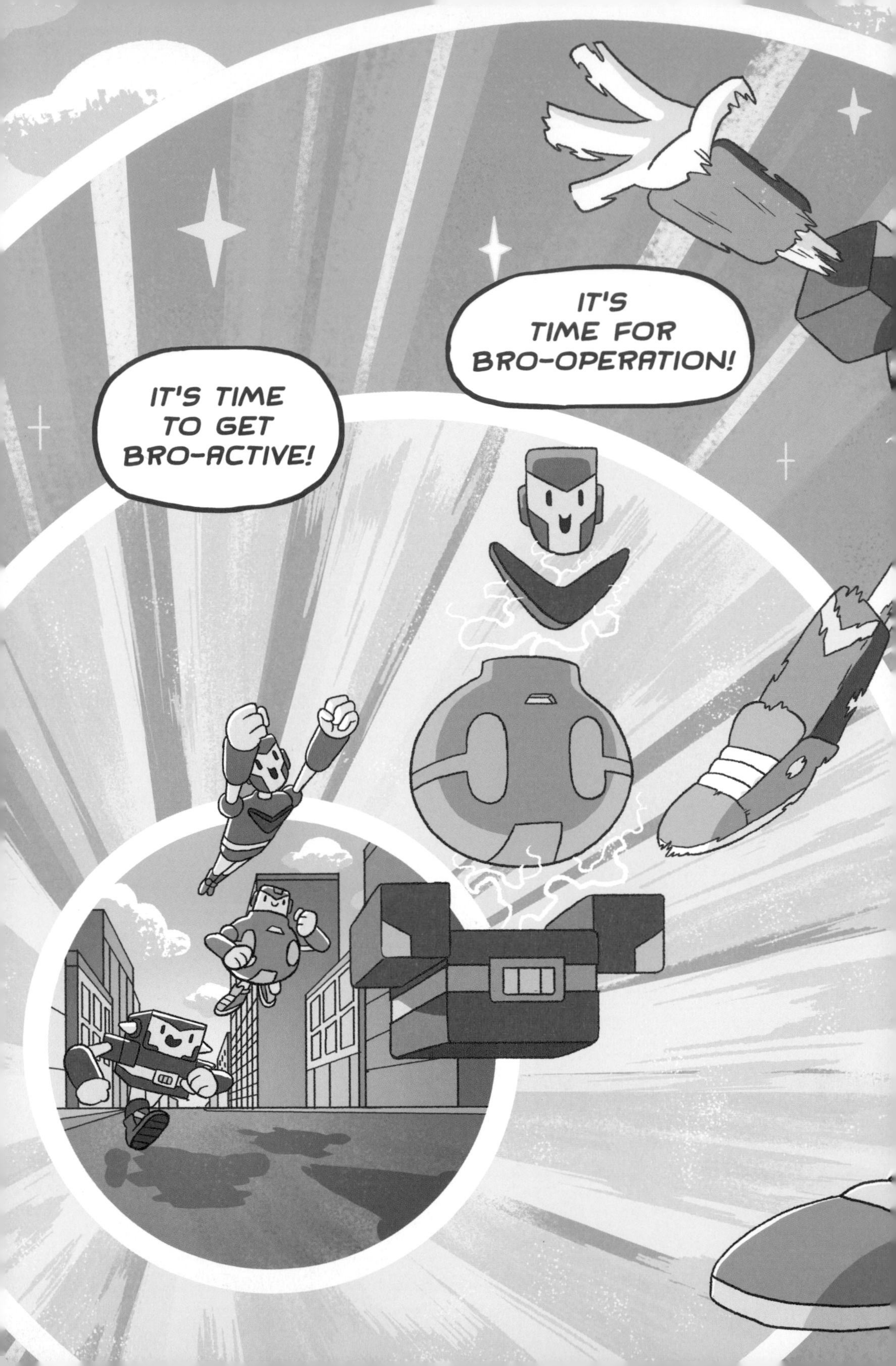
IT'S TIME TO GET BRO-ACTIVE!
IT'S TIME FOR BRO-OPERATION!

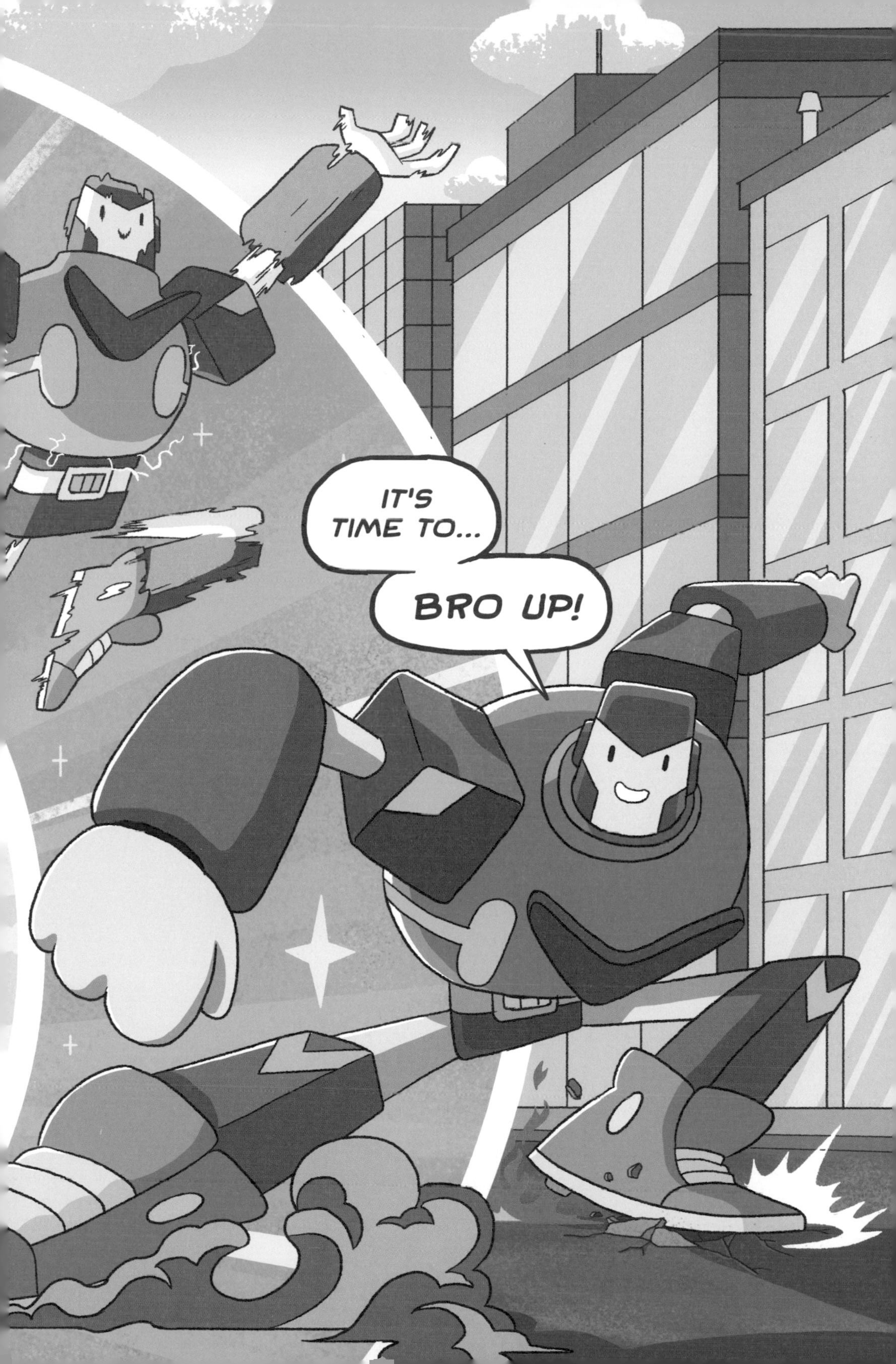
IT'S TIME TO...
BRO UP!

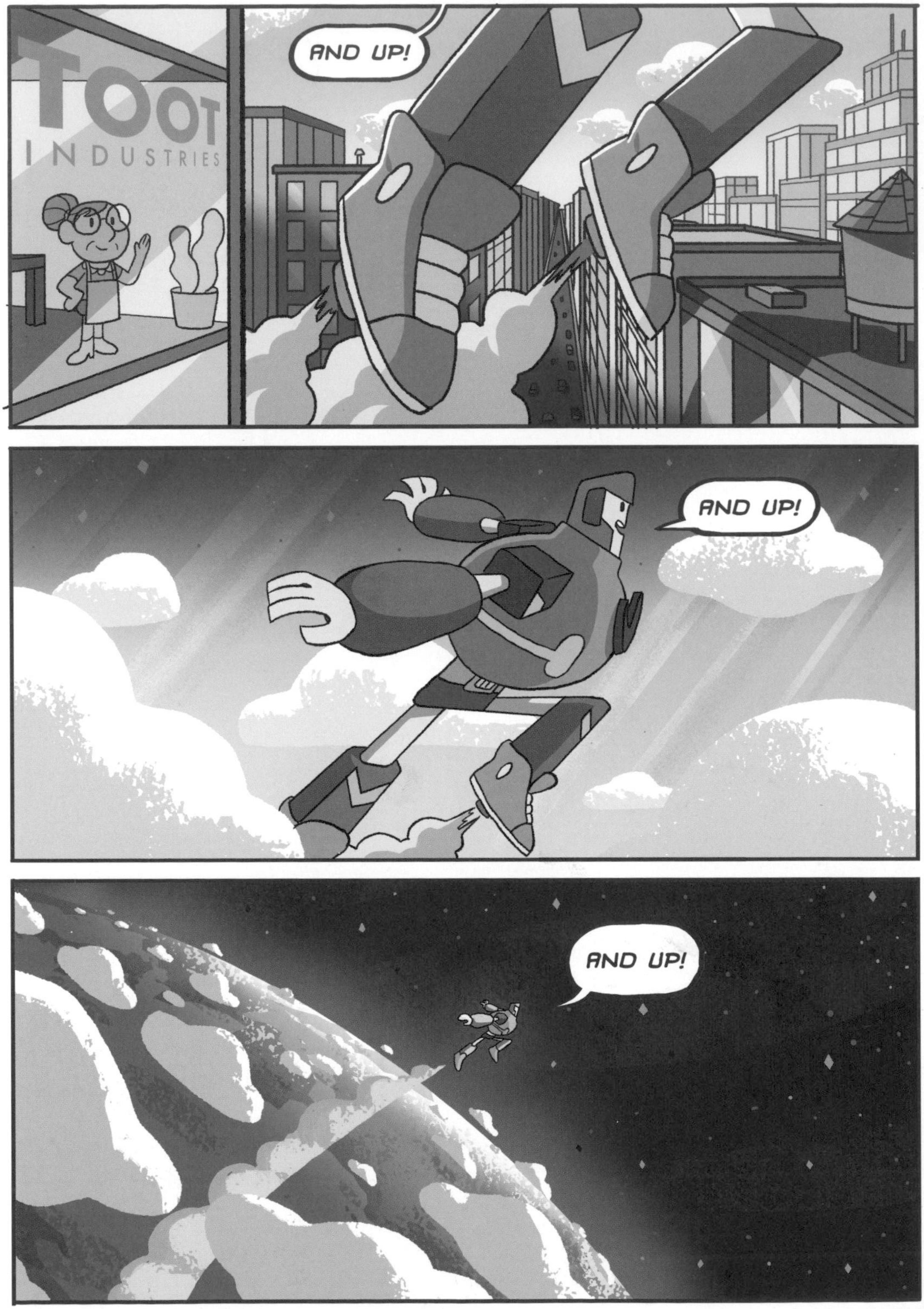
TOOT
INDUSTRIES
AND UP!
AND UP!
AND UP!

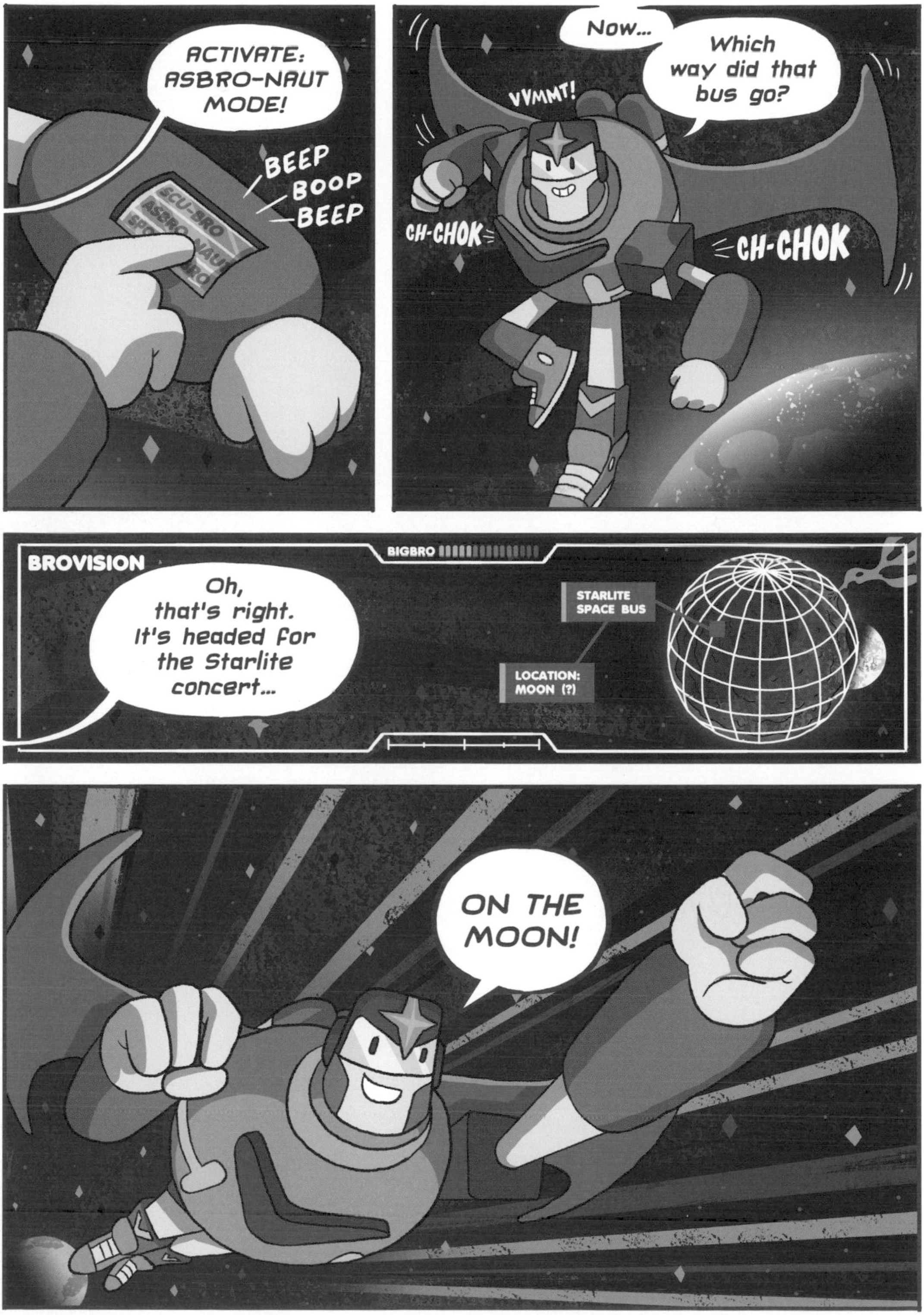
ACTIVATE: ASBRO-NAUT MODE!
BEEP
BOOP
BEEP
Now...
Which way did that bus go?
VVMMT!
CH-CHOK
CH-CHOK
BROVISION
BIGBRO
Oh, that's right. It's headed for the Starlite concert...
STARLITE SPACE BUS
LOCATION: MOON (?)
ON THE MOON!

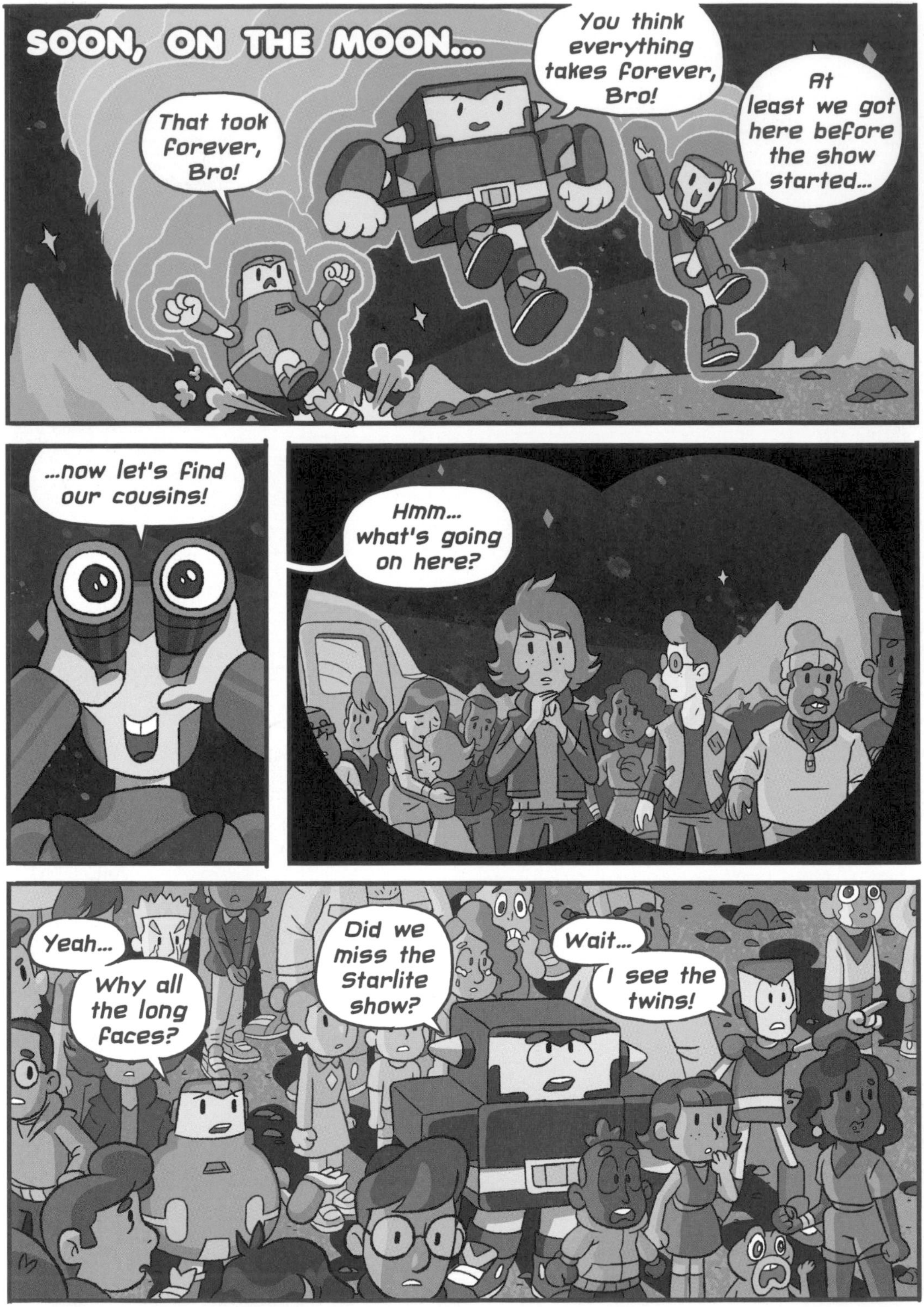
SOON, ON THE MOON...
That took forever, Bro!
You think everything takes forever, Bro!
At least we got here before the show started...
...now let's find our cousins!
Hmm... what's going on here?
Yeah...
Why all the long faces?
Did we miss the Starlite show?
Wait...
I see the twins!

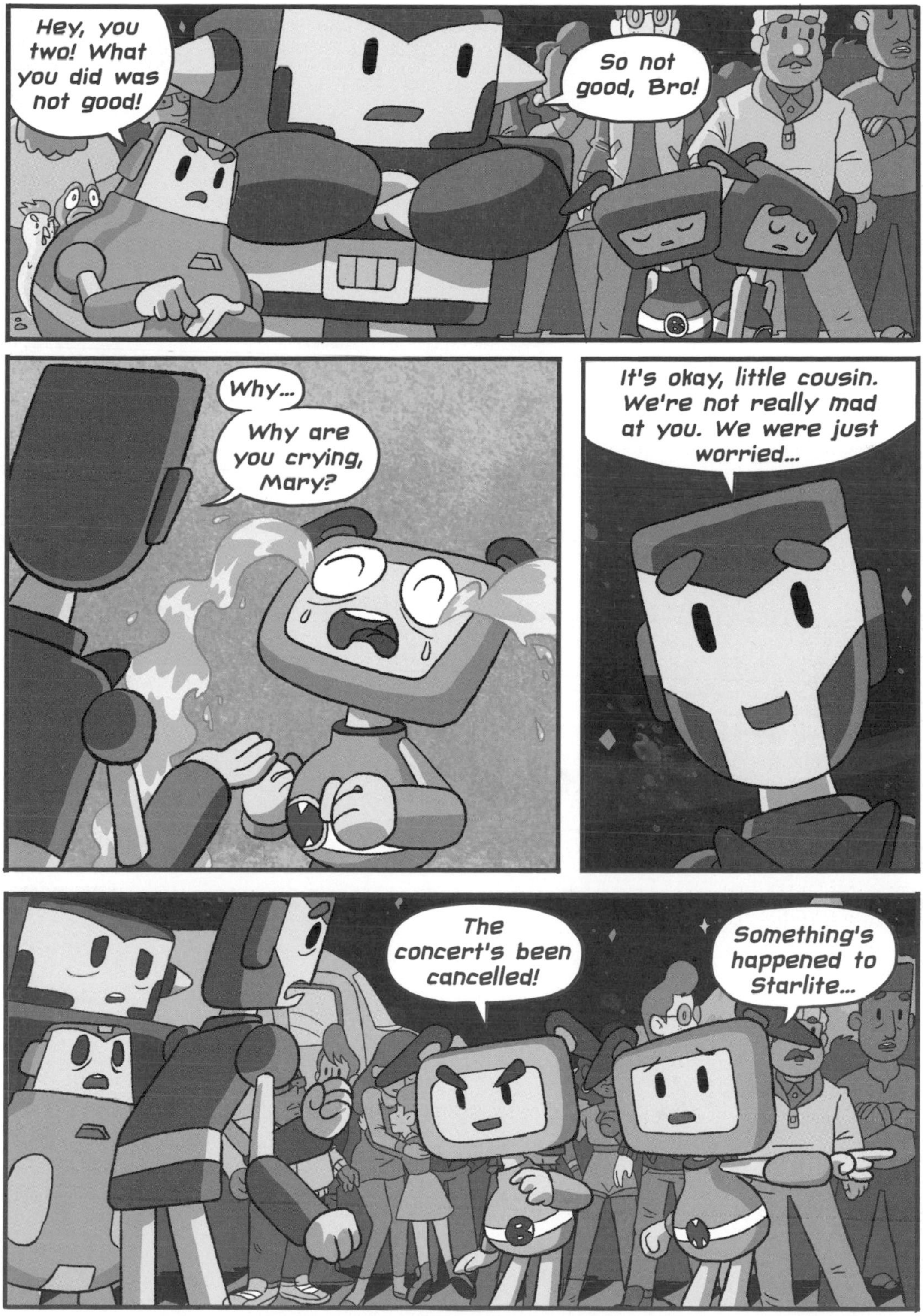
Hey, you two! What you did was not good!
So not good, Bro!
Why...
Why are you crying, Mary?
It's okay, little cousin. We're not really mad at you. We were just worried...
The concert's been cancelled!
Something's happened to Starlite...

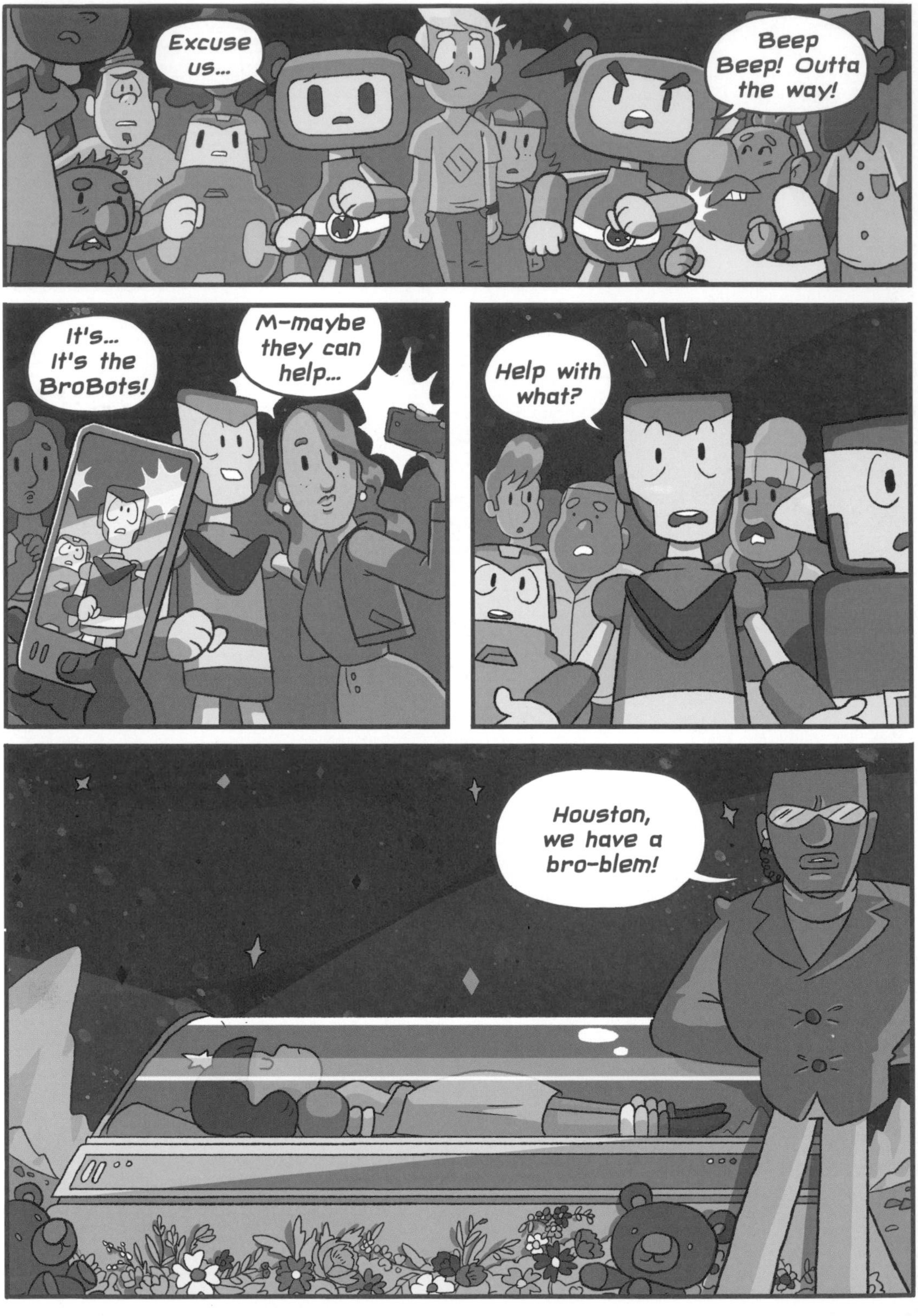
Excuse us...
Beep Beep! Outta the way!
It's... It's the BroBots!
M-maybe they can help...
Help with what?
Houston, we have a bro-blem!

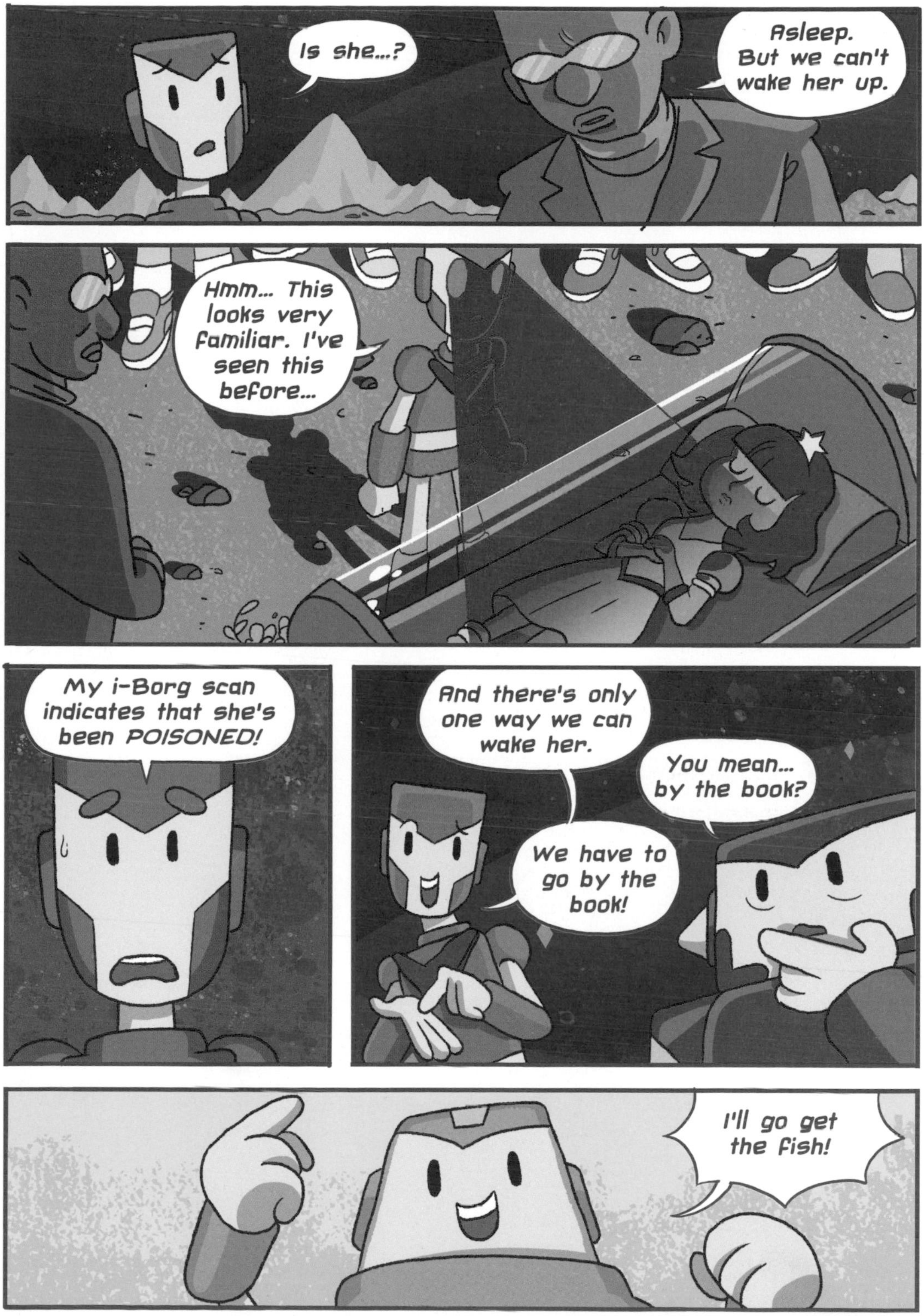
Is she...?
Asleep. But we can't wake her up.
Hmm... This looks very familiar. I've seen this before...
My i-Borg scan indicates that she's been POISONED!
And there's only one way we can wake her.
We have to go by the book!
You mean... by the book?
I'll go get the fish!

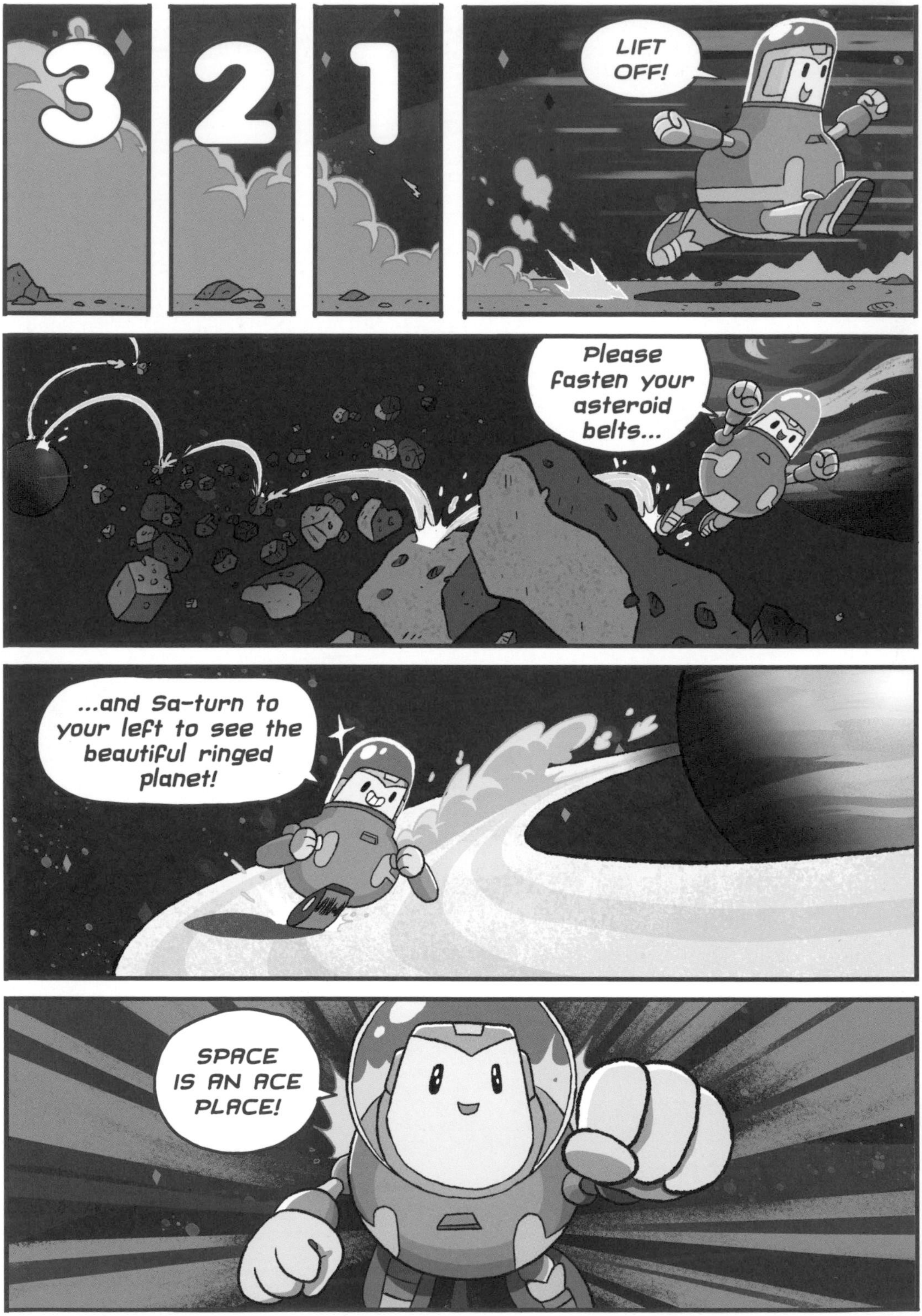
3
2
1
LIFT OFF!
Please fasten your asteroid belts...
...and Sa-turn to your left to see the beautiful ringed planet!
SPACE IS AN ACE PLACE!

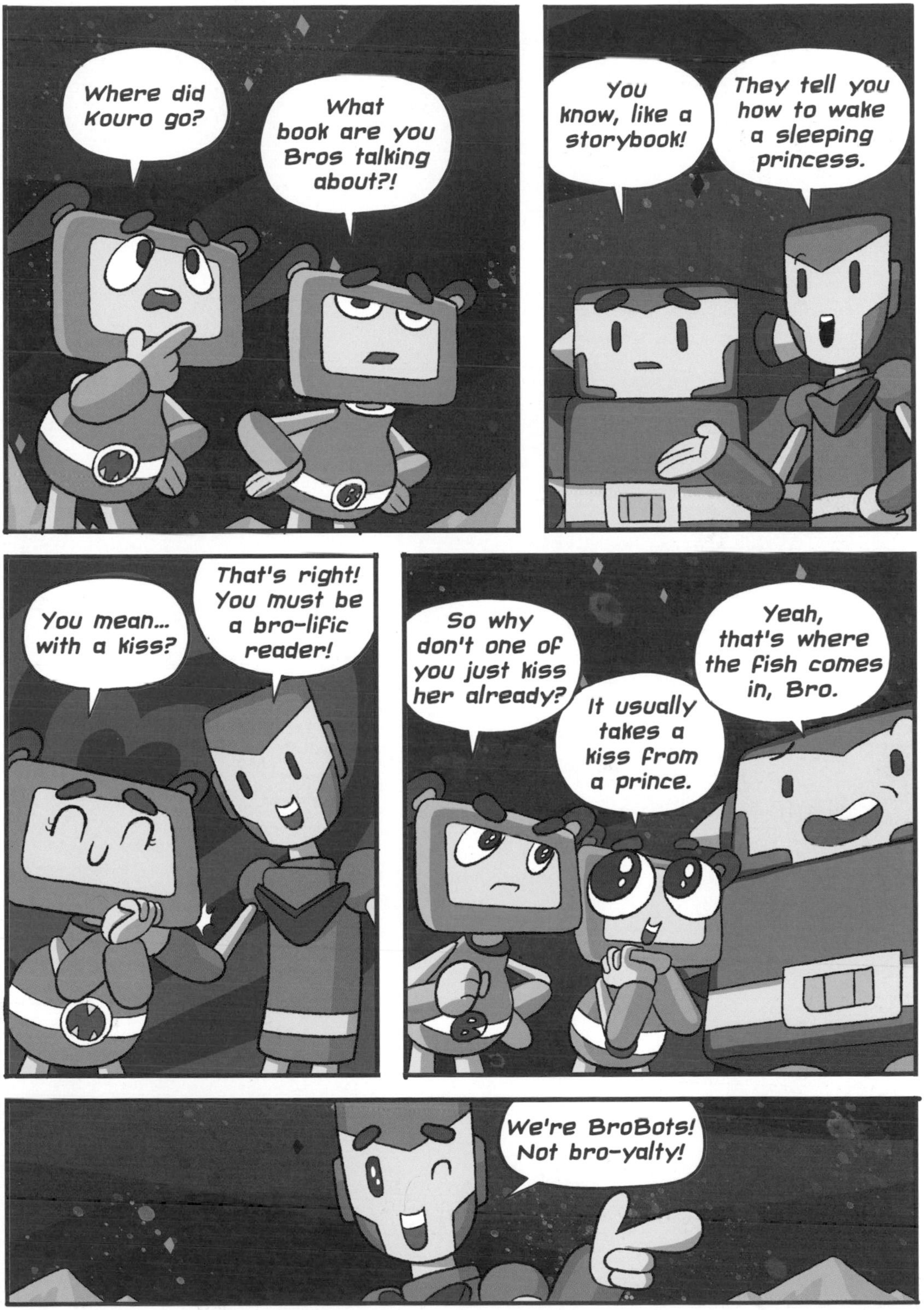
Where did Kouro go?
What book are you Bros talking about?!
You know, like a storybook!
They tell you how to wake a sleeping princess.
You mean... with a kiss?
That's right! You must be a bro-lific reader!
So why don't one of you just kiss her already?
It usually takes a kiss from a prince.
Yeah, that's where the fish comes in, Bro.
We're BroBots! Not bro-yalty!

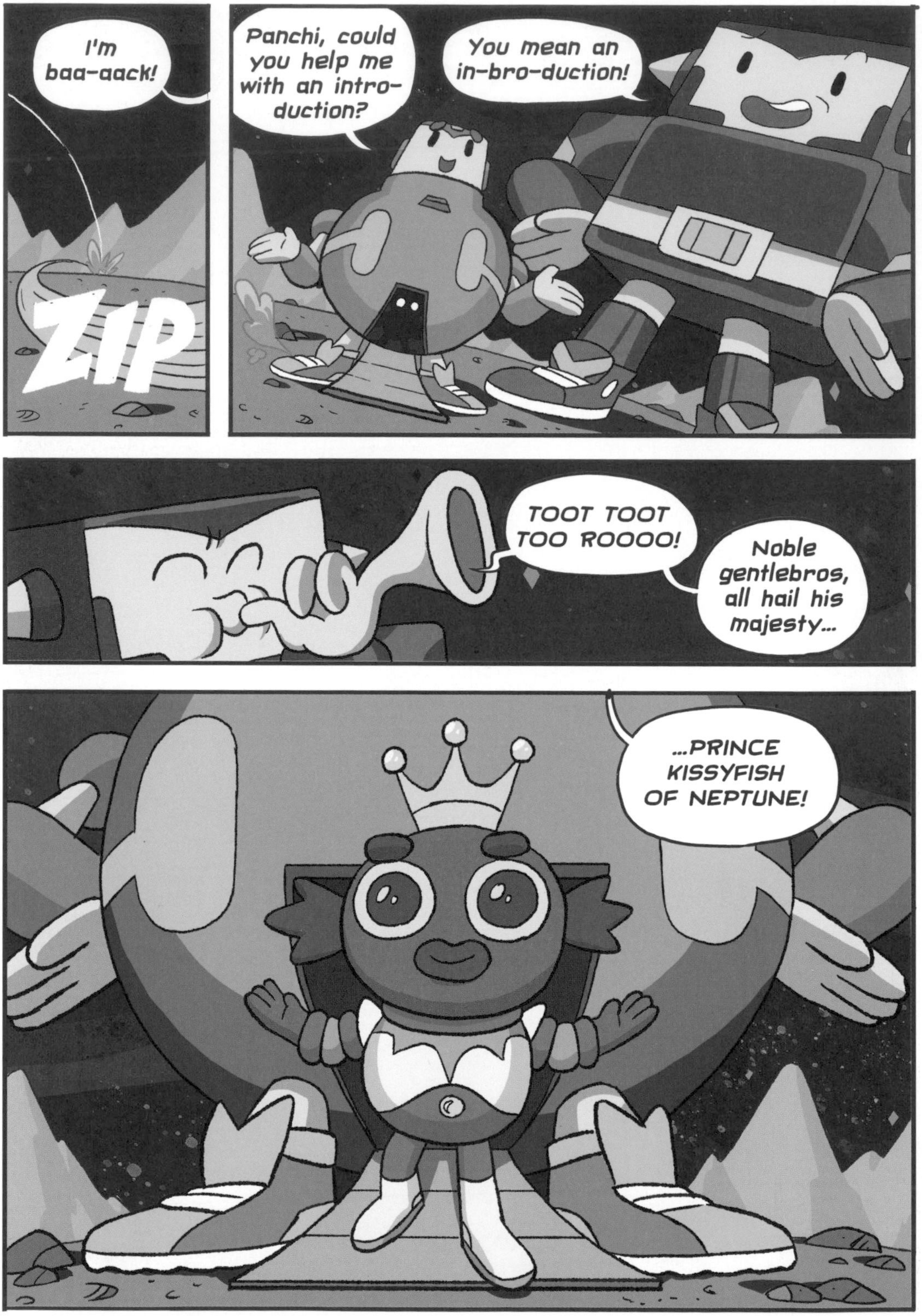
I'm baa-aack!
ZIP
Panchi, could you help me with an intro-duction?
You mean an in-bro-duction!
TOOT TOOT TOO ROOOO!
Noble gentlebros, all hail his majesty...
...PRINCE KISSYFISH OF NEPTUNE!

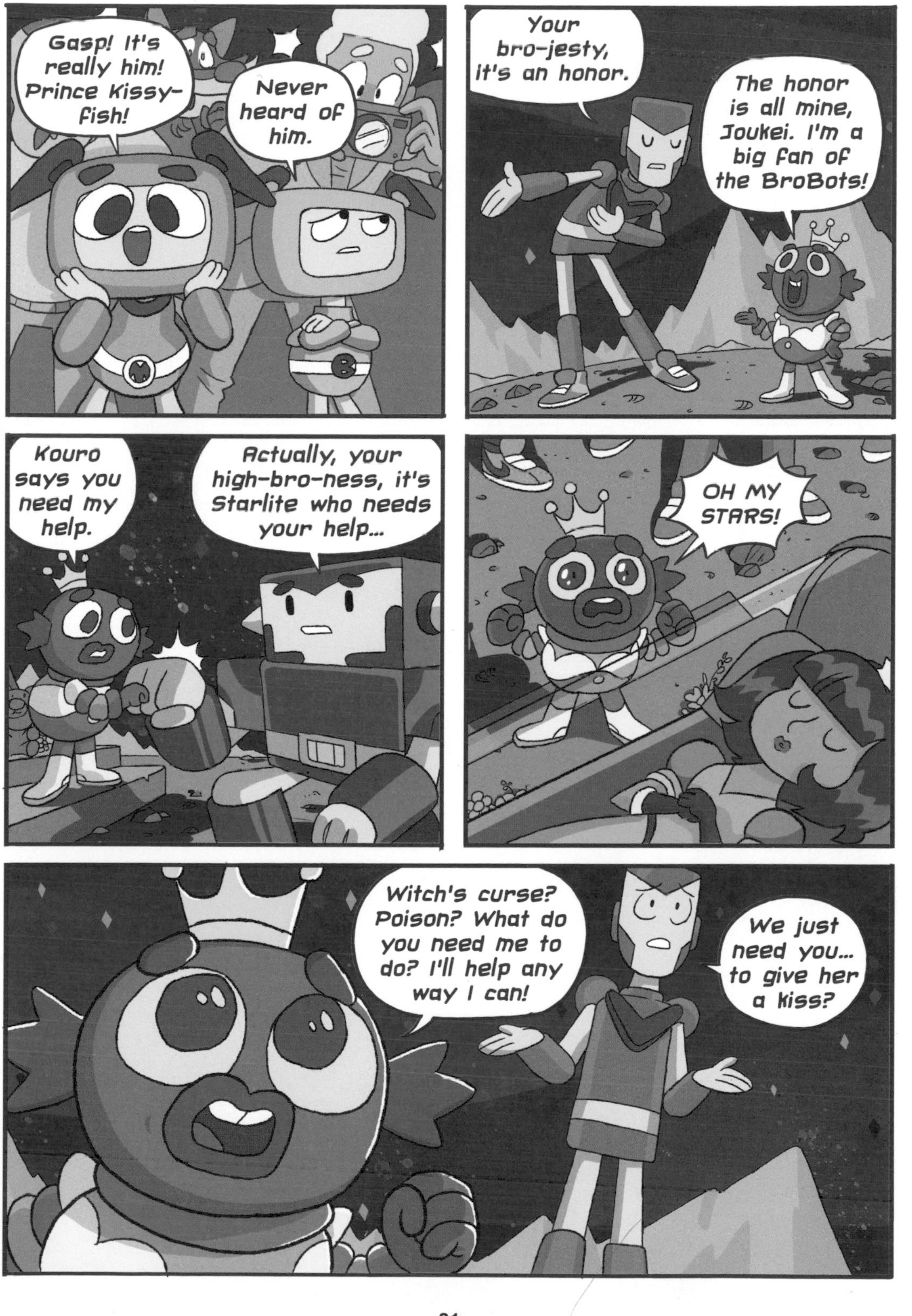
Gasp! It's really him! Prince Kissy-fish!
Never heard of him.
Your bro-jesty, it's an honor.
The honor is all mine, Joukei. I'm a big fan of the BroBots!
Kouro says you need my help.
Actually, your high-bro-ness, it's Starlite who needs your help...
OH MY STARS!
Witch's curse? Poison? What do you need me to do? I'll help any way I can!
We just need you... to give her a kiss?

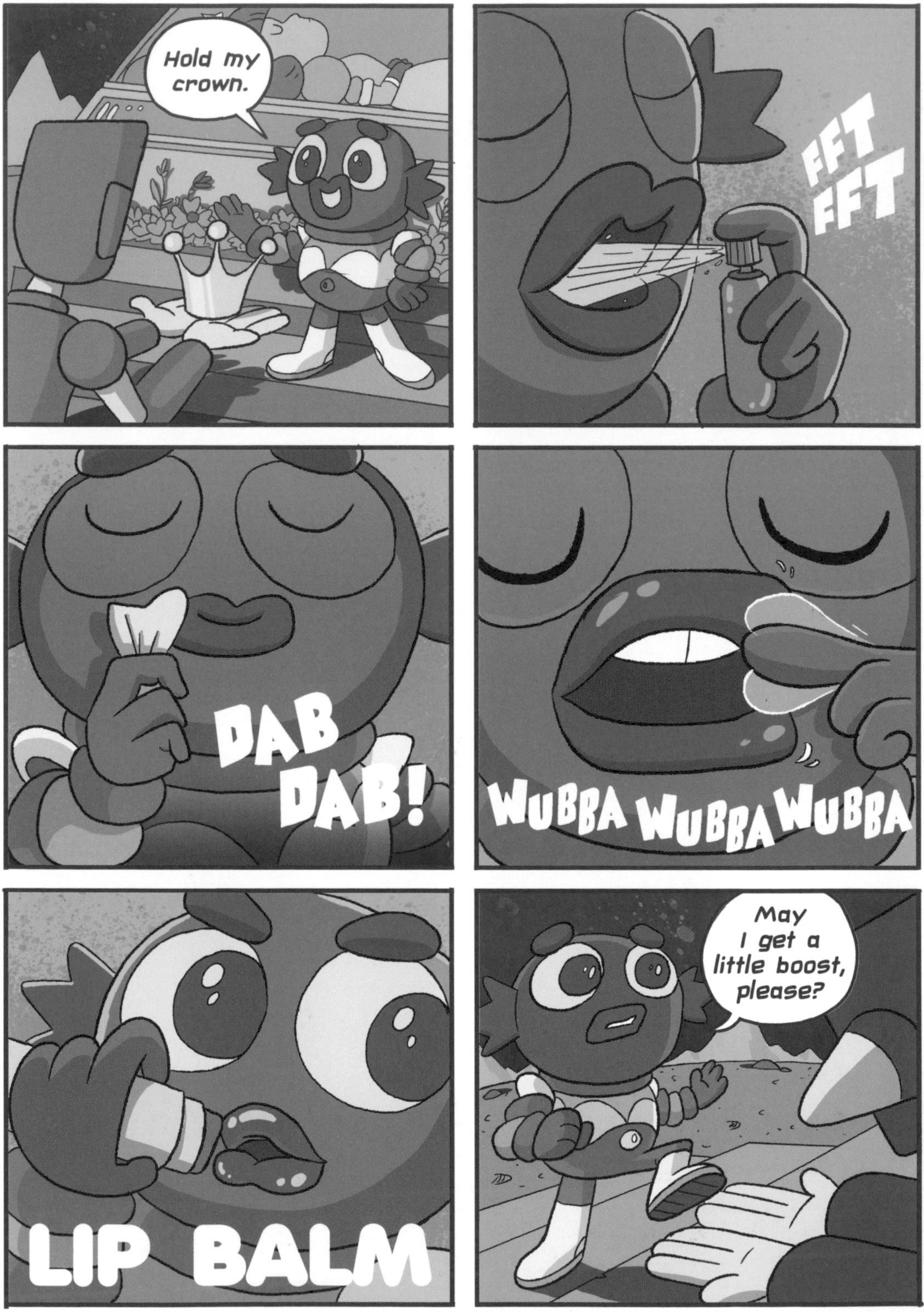
Hold my crown.
FFT FFT
DAB DAB!
WUBBA WUBBA WUBBA
LIP BALM
May I get a little boost, please?

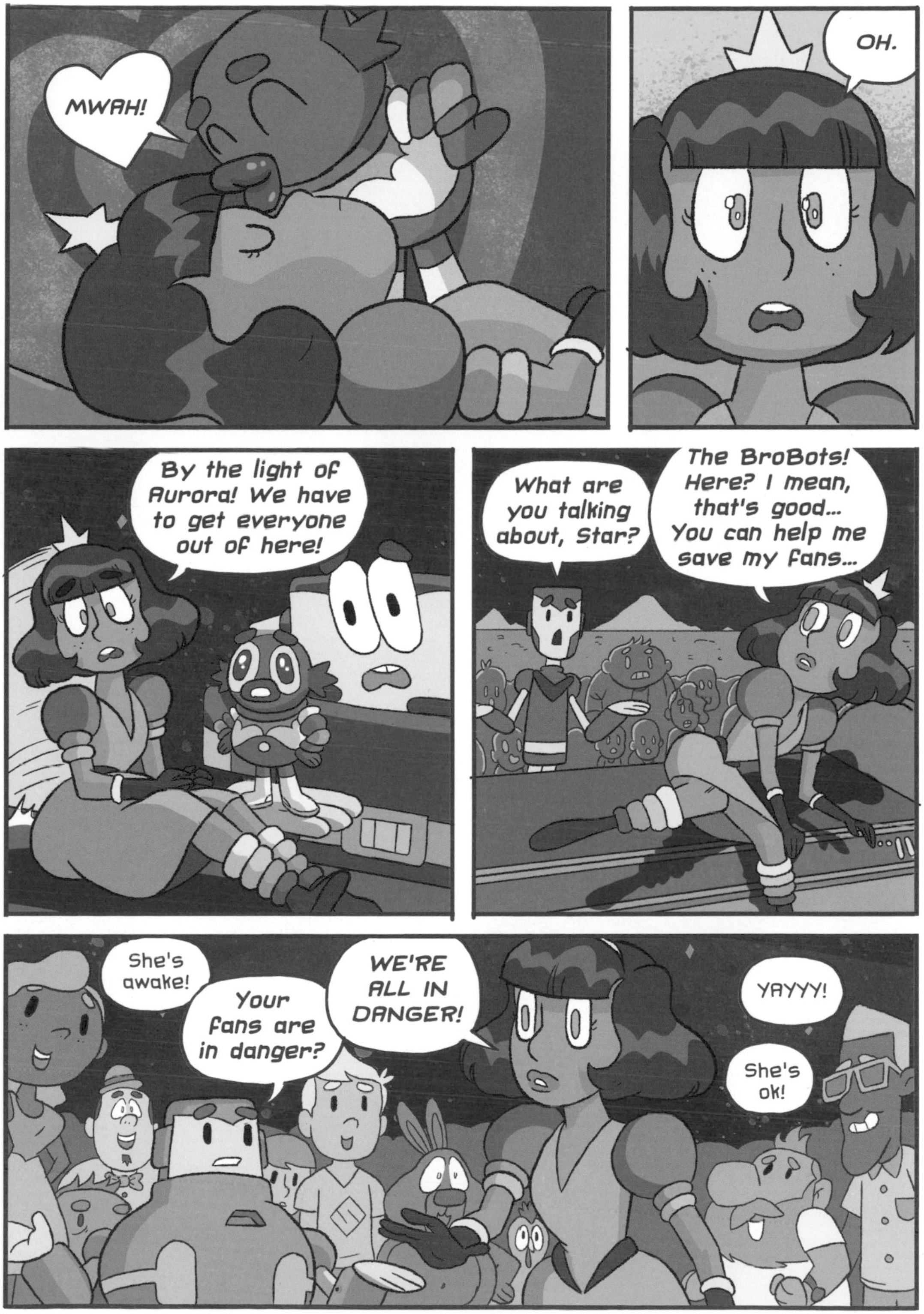
MWAH!
OH.
By the light of Aurora! We have to get everyone out of here!
What are you talking about, Star?
The BroBots! Here? I mean, that's good... You can help me save my fans...
She's awake!
Your fans are in danger?
WE'RE ALL IN DANGER!
YAYYY!
She's ok!

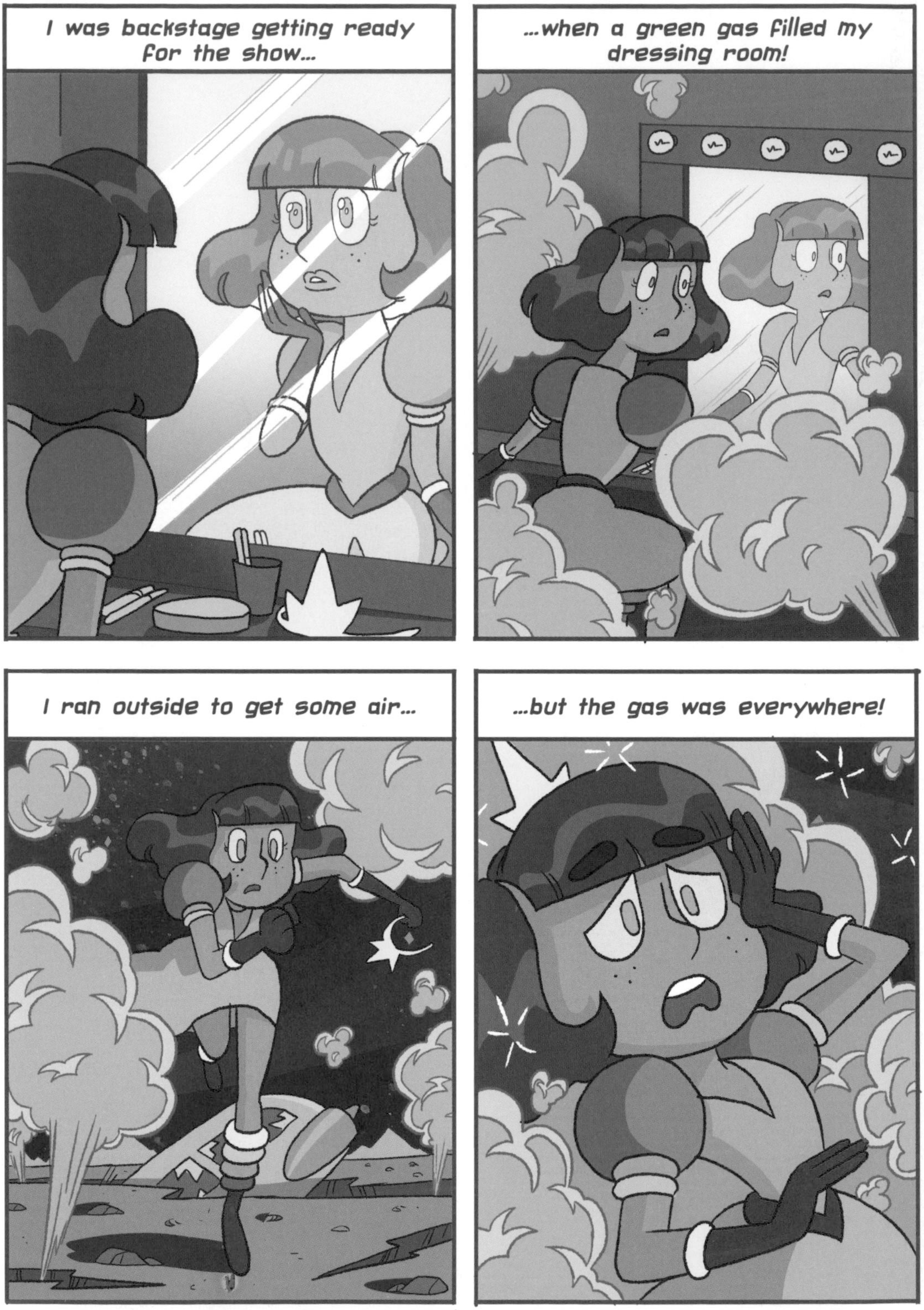
I was backstage getting ready for the show...
...when a green gas filled my dressing room!
I ran outside to get some air...
...but the gas was everywhere!

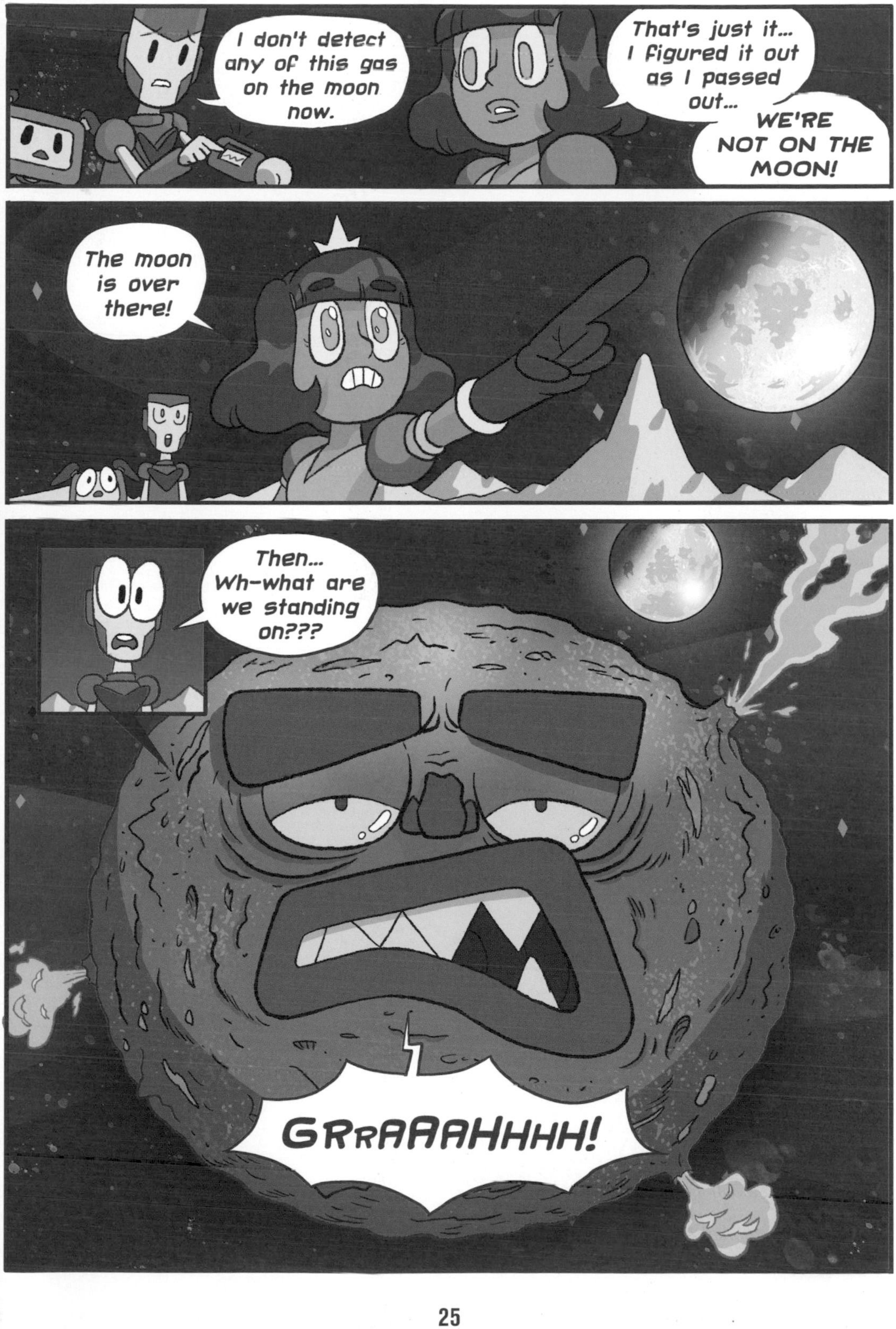
I don't detect any of this gas on the moon now.
That's just it... I figured it out as I passed out...
WE'RE NOT ON THE MOON!
The moon is over there!
Then... Wh-what are we standing on???
GRrRAAAHHHH!

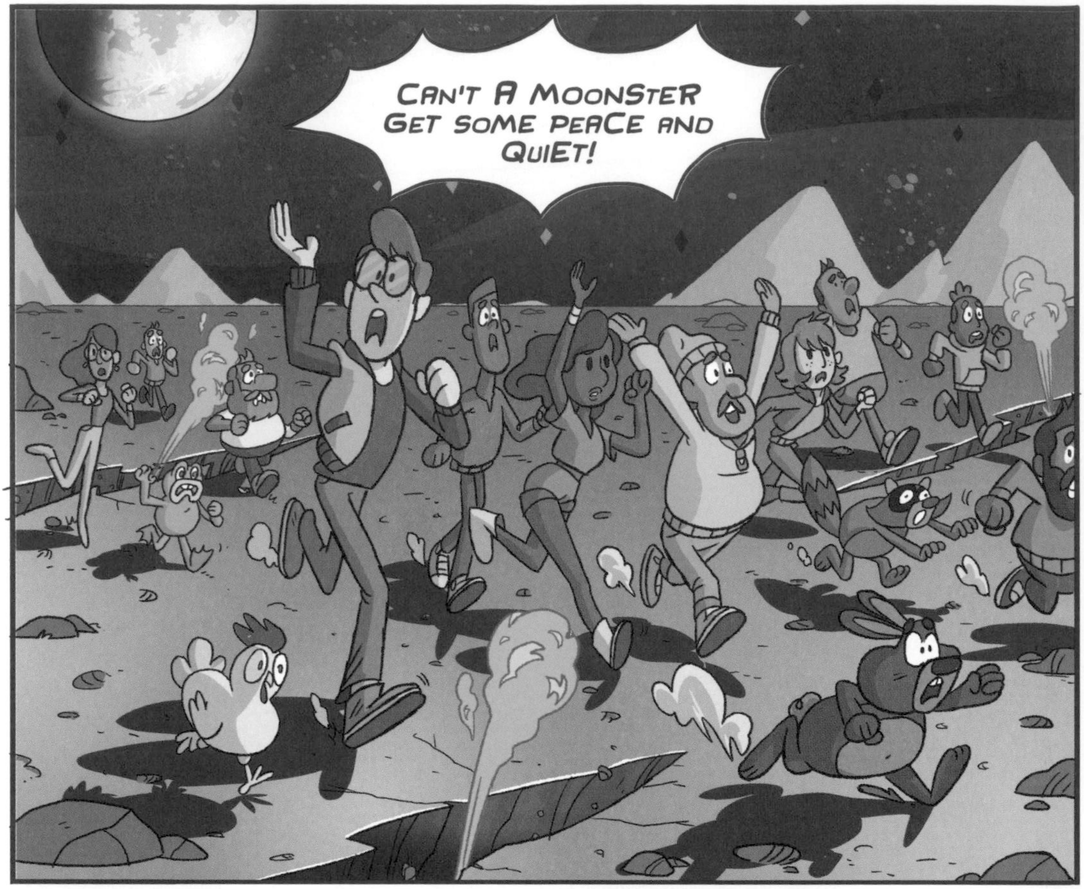
CAN'T A MOONSTER GET SOME PEACE AND QUIET!

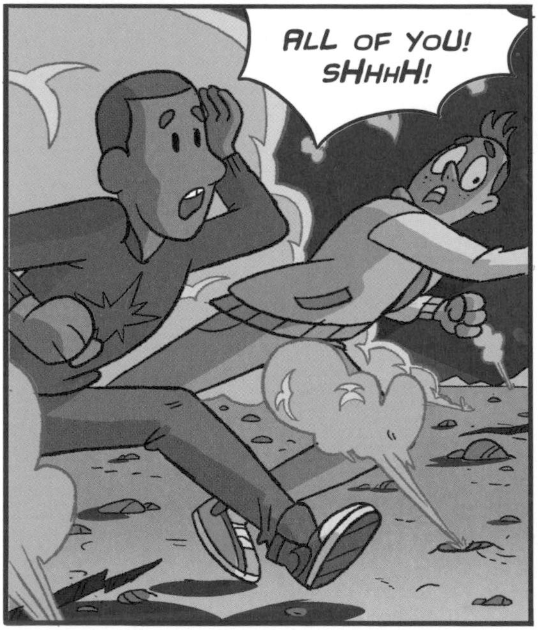
ALL OF YOU! SHHHH!

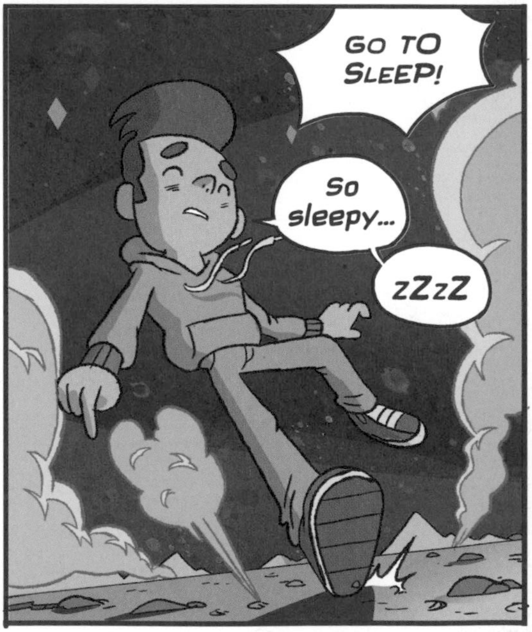
GO TO SLEEP!
So sleepy...
zZzZ

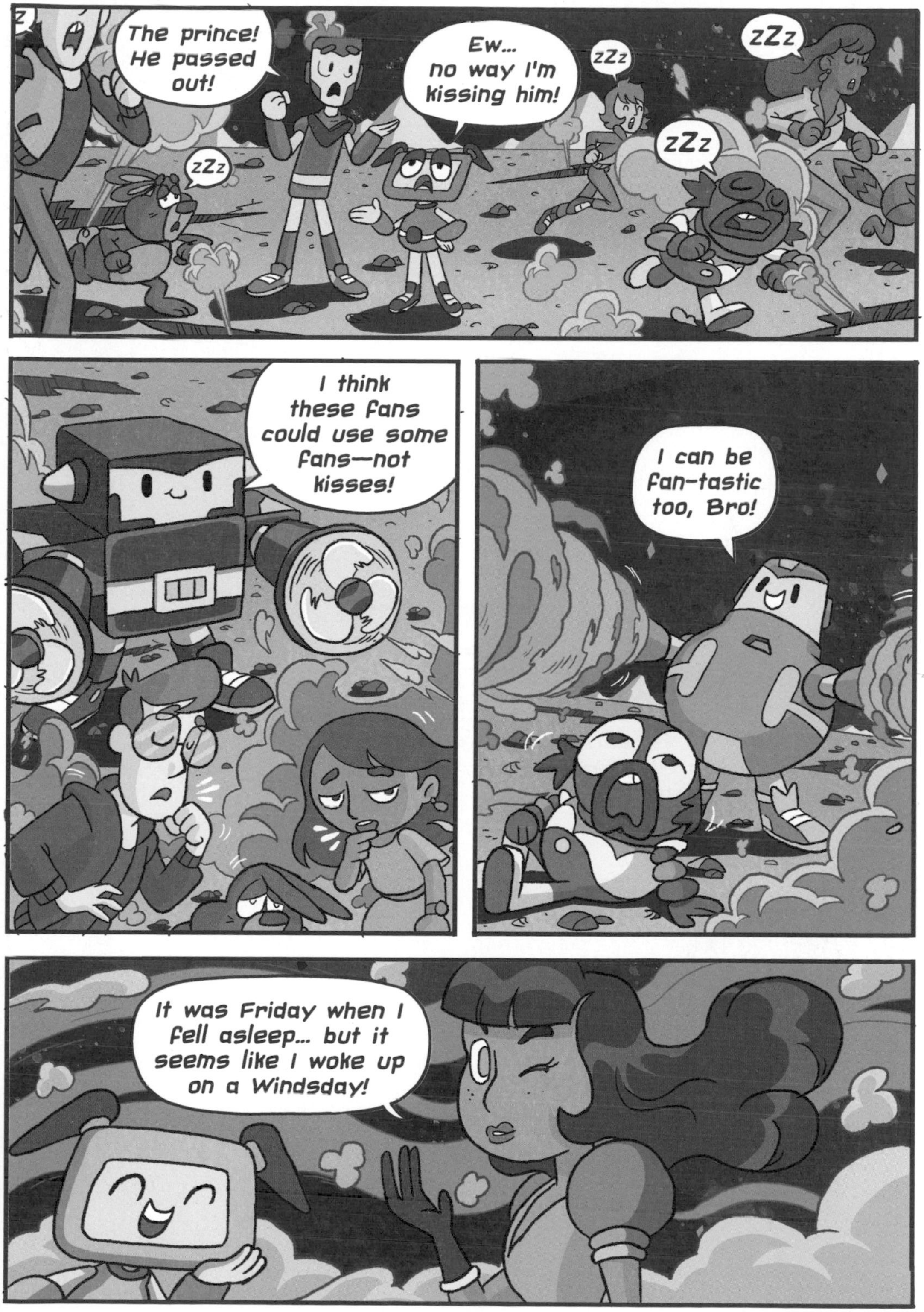
The prince! He passed out!
Ew... no way I'm kissing him!
zZz
zZz
zZz
zZz
I think these fans could use some fans—not kisses!
I can be fan-tastic too, Bro!
It was Friday when I fell asleep... but it seems like I woke up on a Windsday!

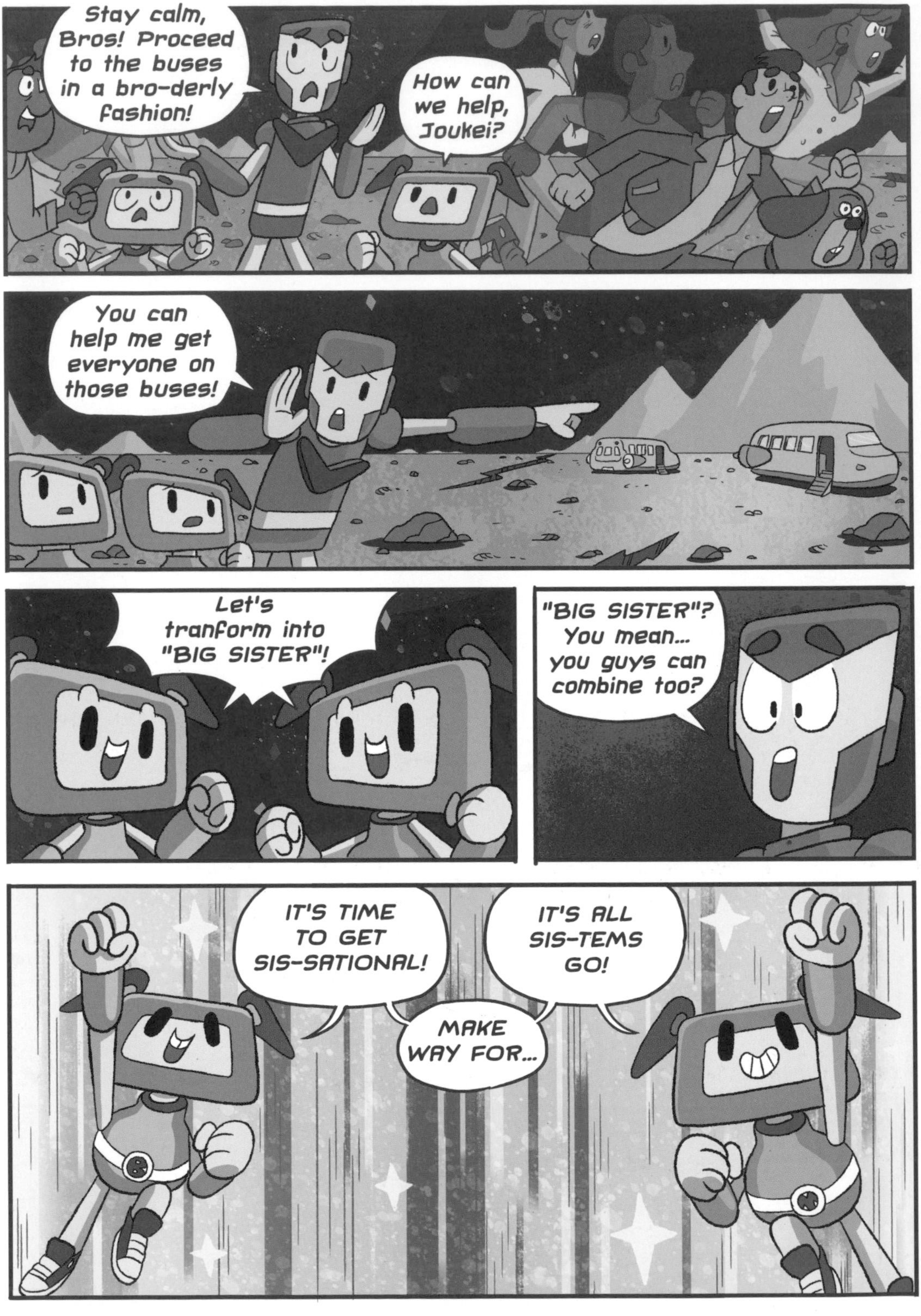
Stay calm, Bros! Proceed to the buses in a bro-derly fashion!
How can we help, Joukei?
You can help me get everyone on those buses!
Let's tranform into "BIG SISTER"!
"BIG SISTER"? You mean... you guys can combine too?
IT'S TIME TO GET SIS-SATIONAL!
IT'S ALL SIS-TEMS GO!
MAKE WAY FOR...

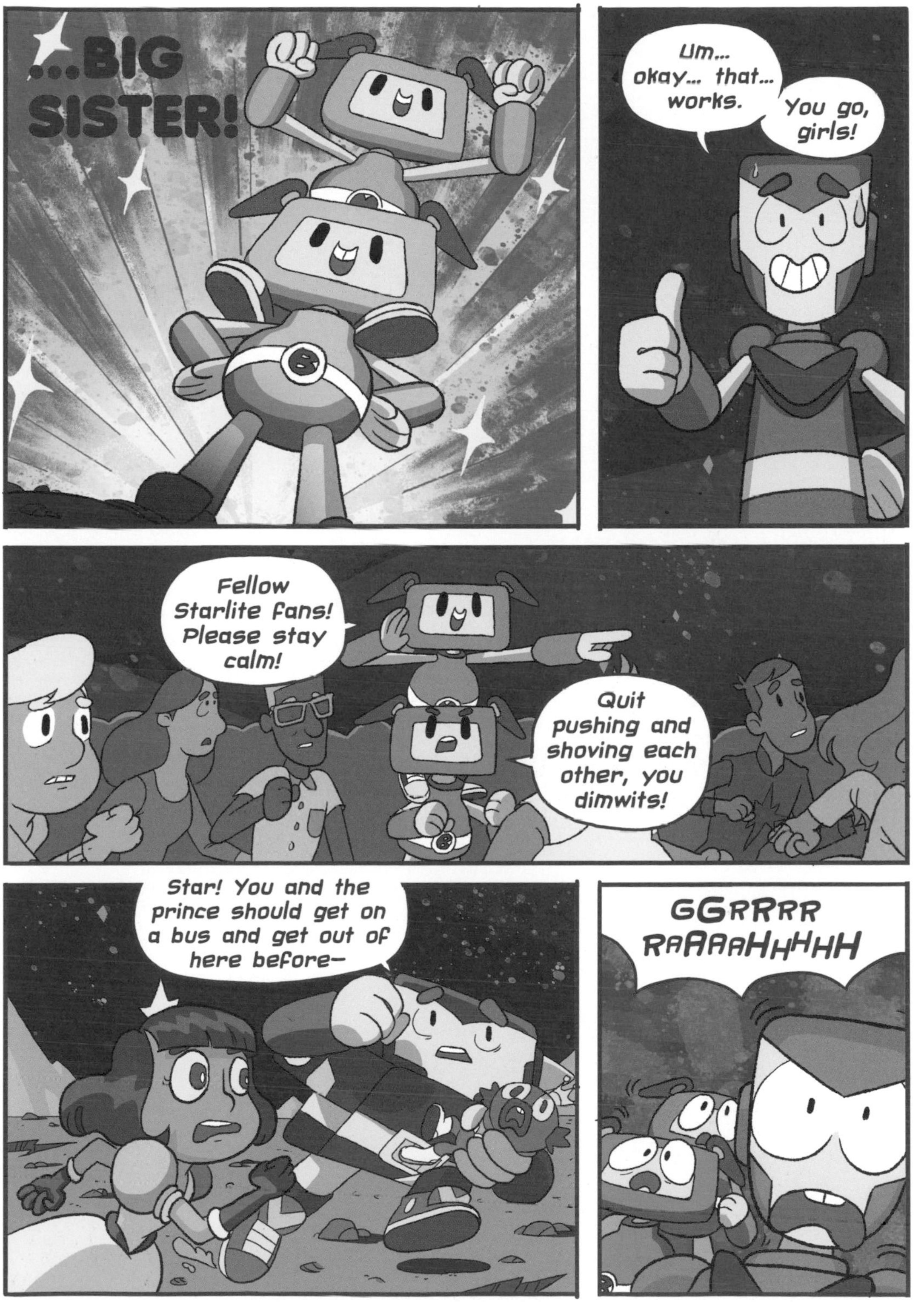
...BIG SISTER!
Um... okay... that... works.
You go, girls!
Fellow Starlite fans! Please stay calm!
Quit pushing and shoving each other, you dimwits!
Star! You and the prince should get on a bus and get out of here before—
GGRRRR RAAAAHHHHH

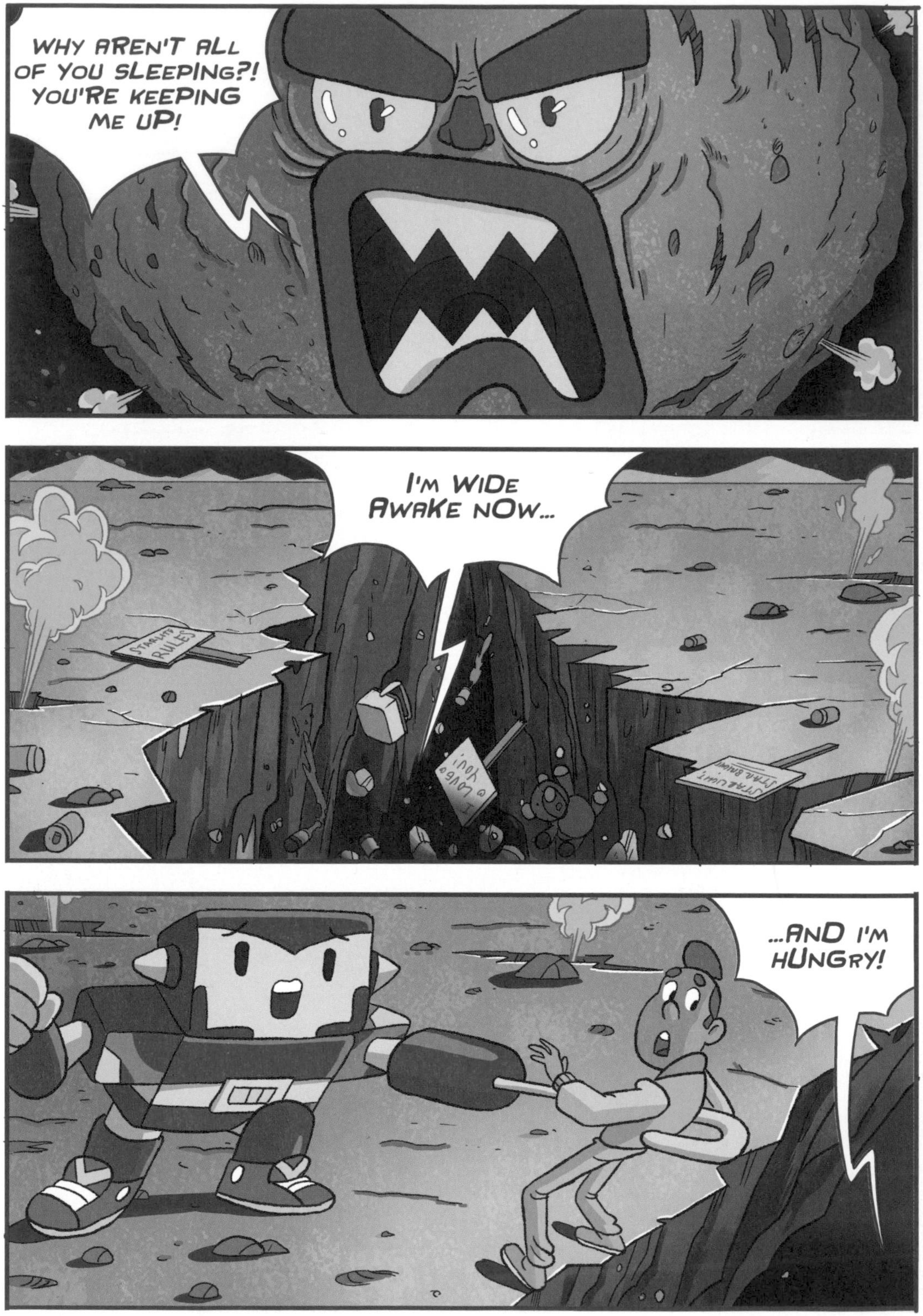
WHY AREN'T ALL OF YOU SLEEPING?! YOU'RE KEEPING ME UP!
I'M WIDE AWAKE NOW...
...AND I'M HUNGRY!

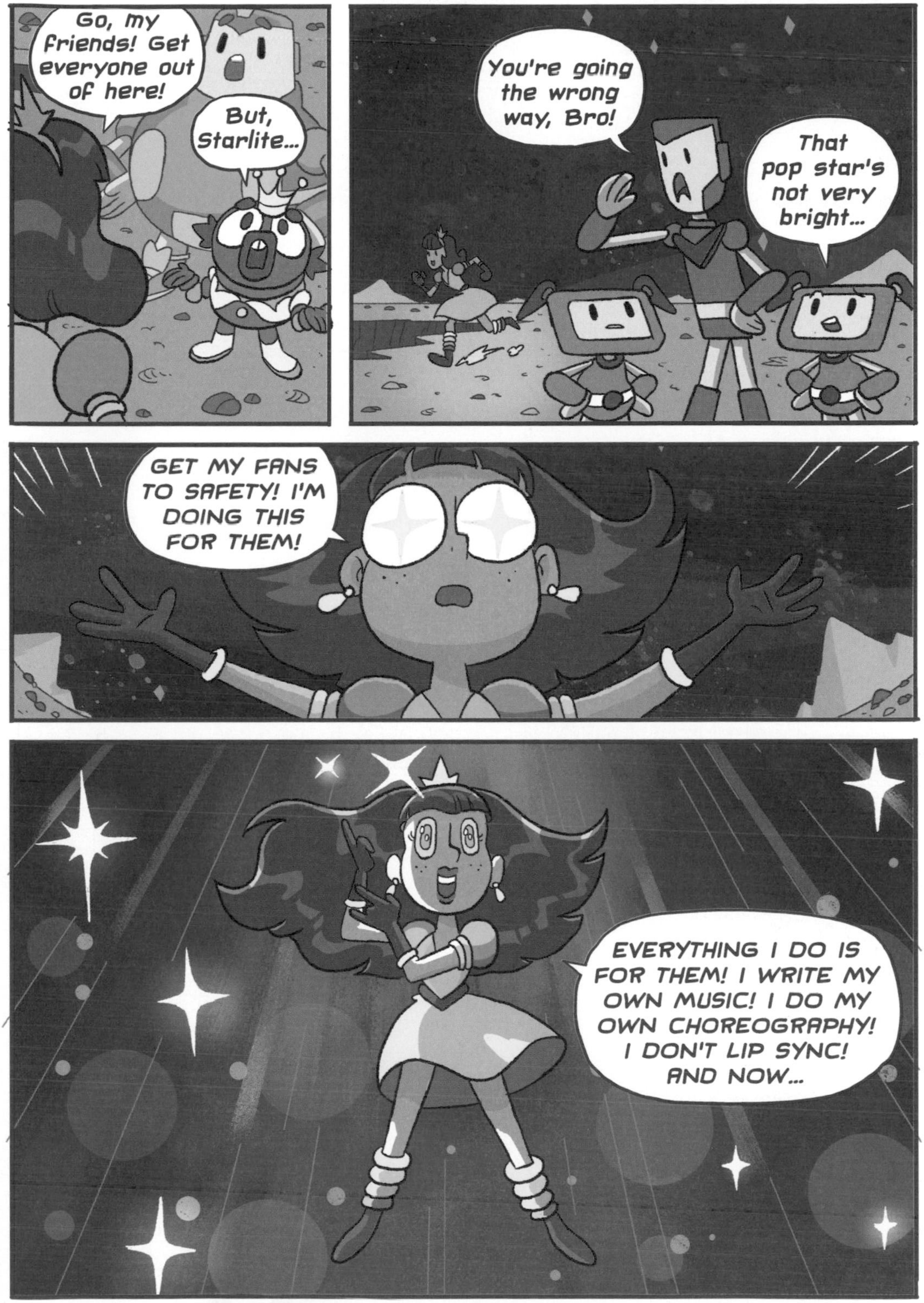
Go, my friends! Get everyone out of here!
But, Starlite...
You're going the wrong way, Bro!
That pop star's not very bright...
GET MY FANS TO SAFETY! I'M DOING THIS FOR THEM!
EVERYTHING I DO IS FOR THEM! I WRITE MY OWN MUSIC! I DO MY OWN CHOREOGRAPHY! I DON'T LIP SYNC! AND NOW...

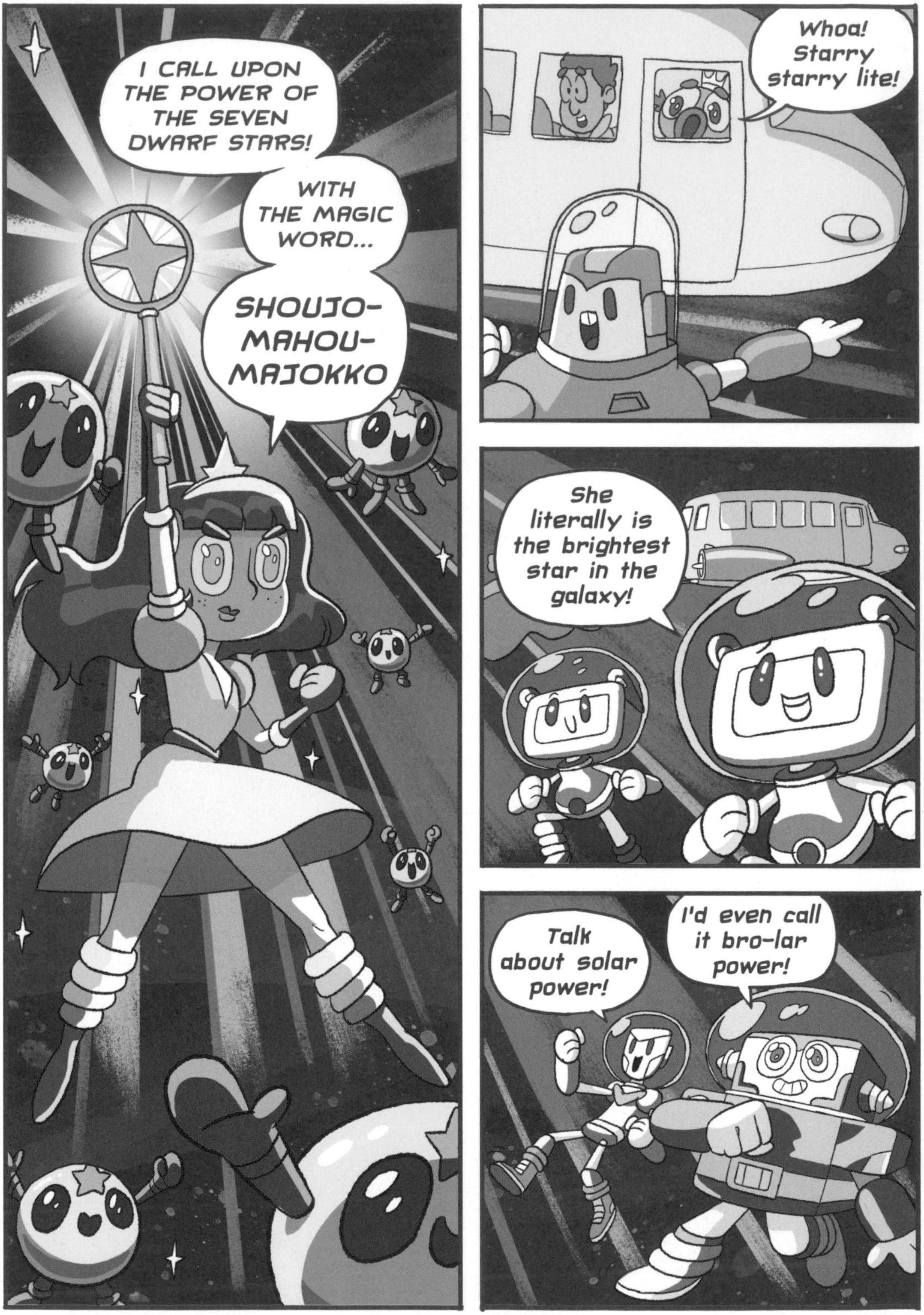
I CALL UPON THE POWER OF THE SEVEN DWARF STARS!
WITH THE MAGIC WORD...
SHOUJO-MAHOU-MAJOKKO
Whoa! Starry starry lite!
She literally is the brightest star in the galaxy!
Talk about solar power!
I'd even call it bro-lar power!

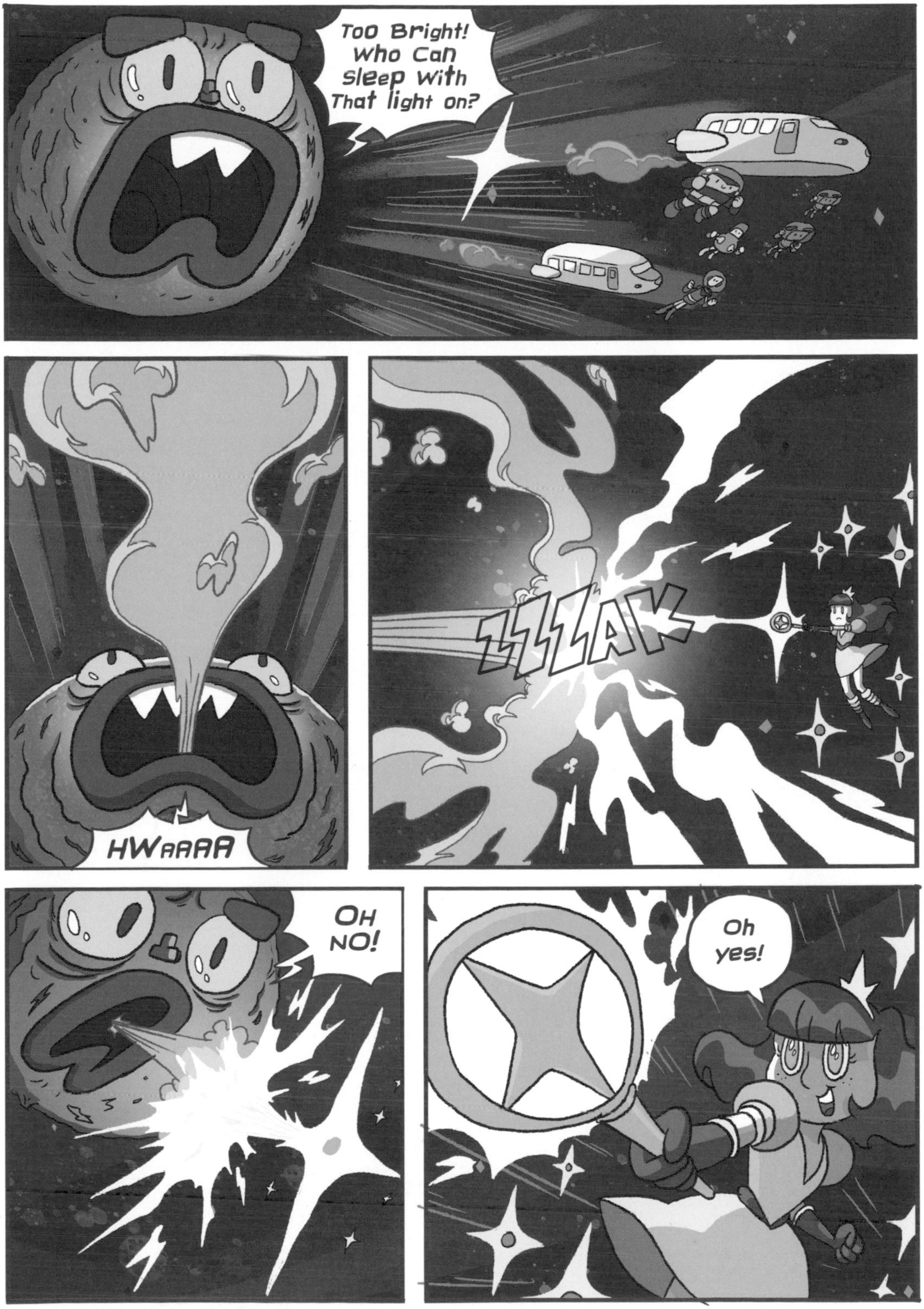
Too Bright! Who Can sleep with That light on?
HWaaaa
ZZZAK
OH NO!
Oh yes!

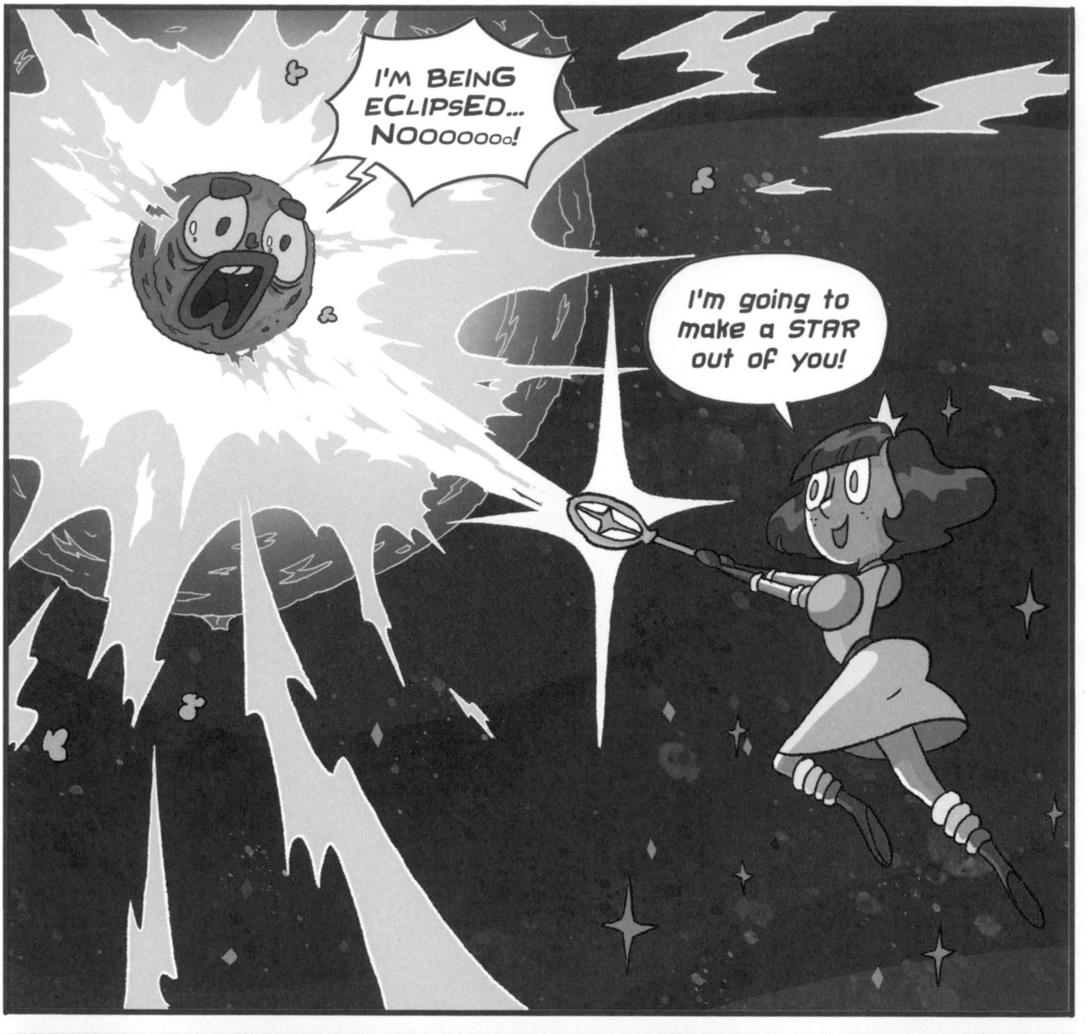
I'M BEING ECLIPSED... NOoooooo!
I'm going to make a STAR out of you!

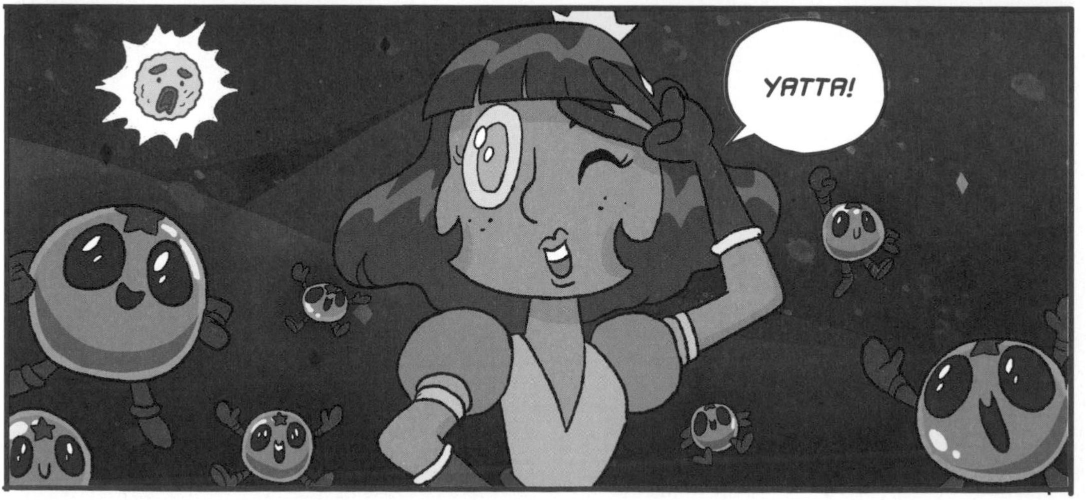
YATTA!

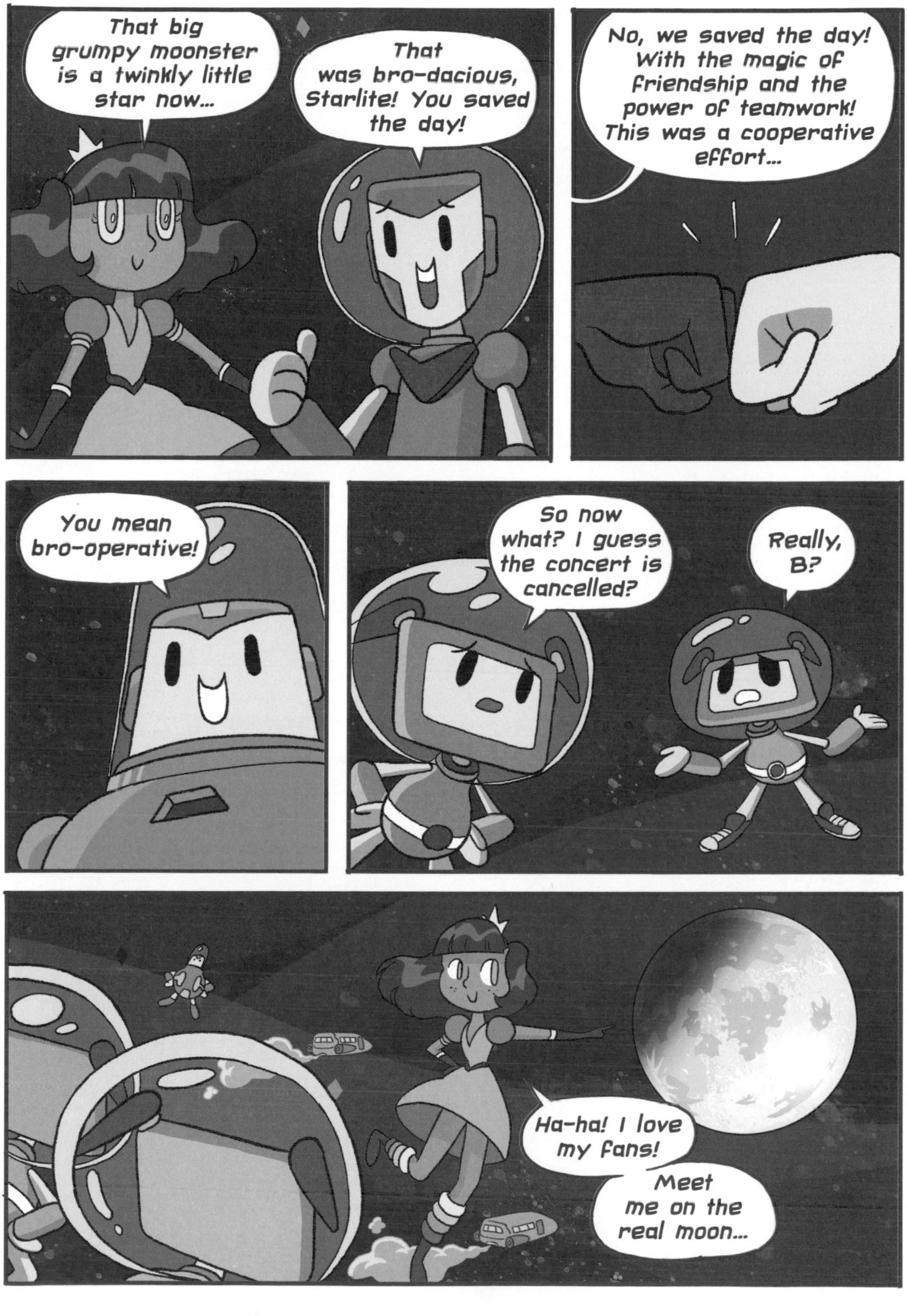
That big grumpy moonster is a twinkly little star now...
That was bro-dacious, Starlite! You saved the day!
No, we saved the day! With the magic of friendship and the power of teamwork! This was a cooperative effort...
You mean bro-operative!
So now what? I guess the concert is cancelled?
Really, B?
Ha-ha! I love my fans!
Meet me on the real moon...

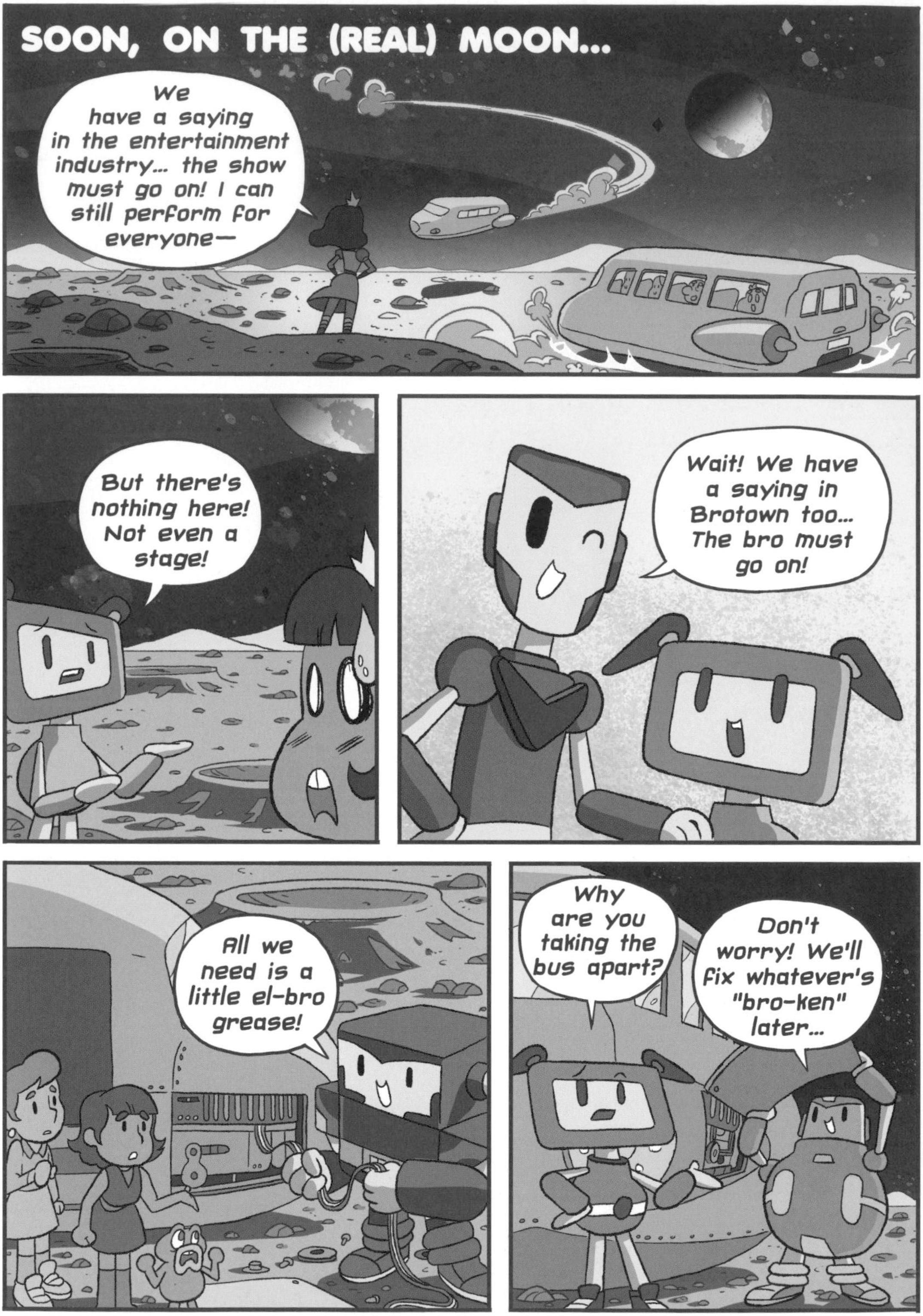
SOON, ON THE (REAL) MOON...
We have a saying in the entertainment industry... the show must go on! I can still perform for everyone—
But there's nothing here! Not even a stage!
Wait! We have a saying in Brotown too... The bro must go on!
All we need is a little el-bro grease!
Why are you taking the bus apart?
Don't worry! We'll fix whatever's "bro-ken" later...

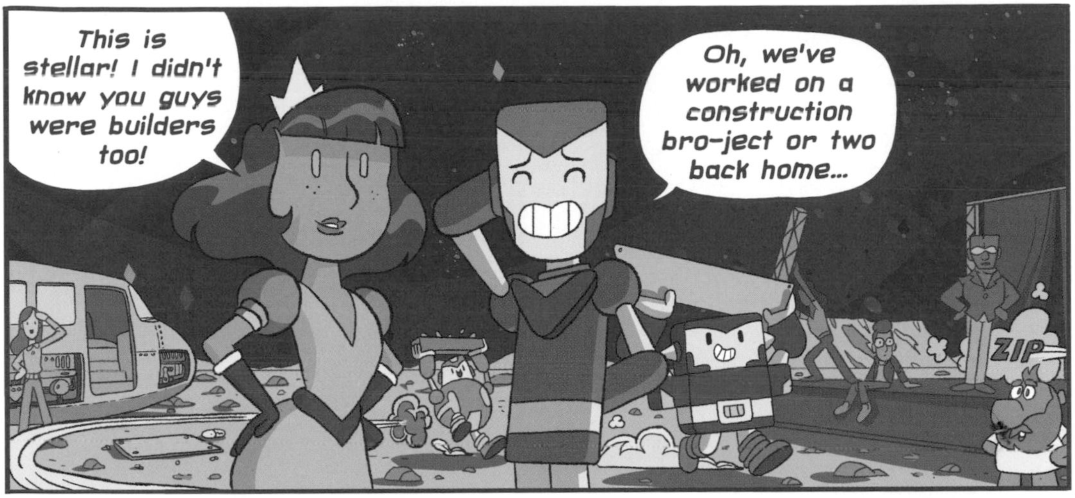
This is stellar! I didn't know you guys were builders too!
Oh, we've worked on a construction bro-ject or two back home...
ZIP

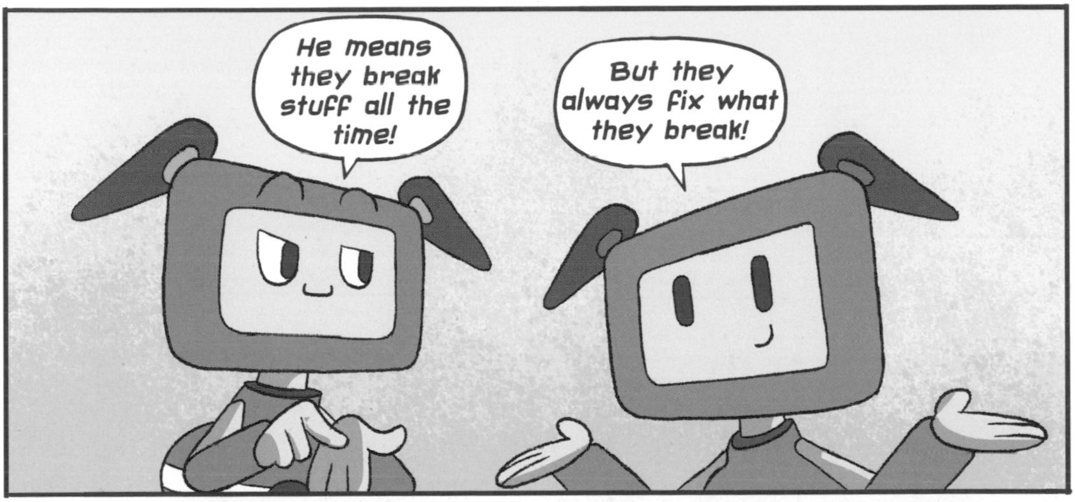
He means they break stuff all the time!
But they always fix what they break!

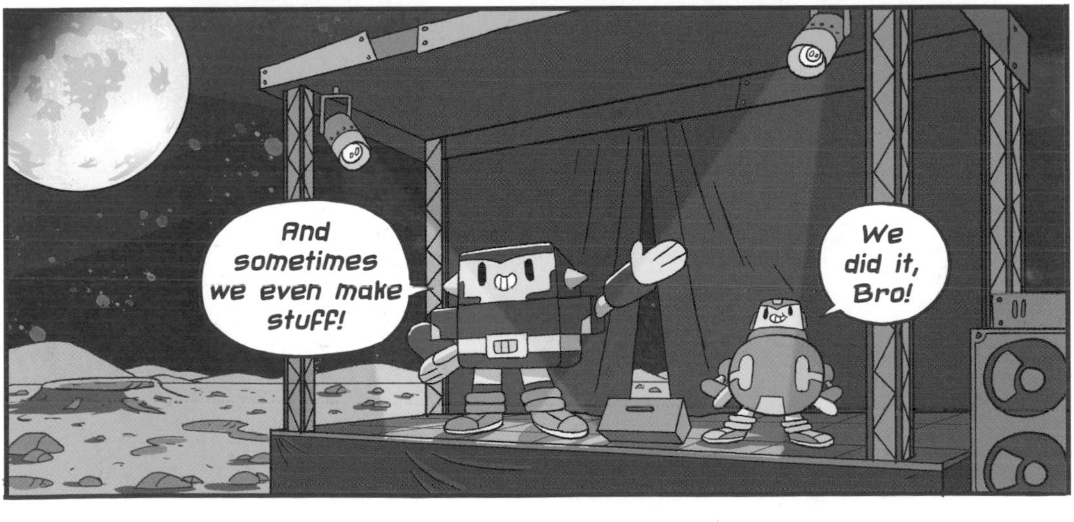
And sometimes we even make stuff!
We did it, Bro!

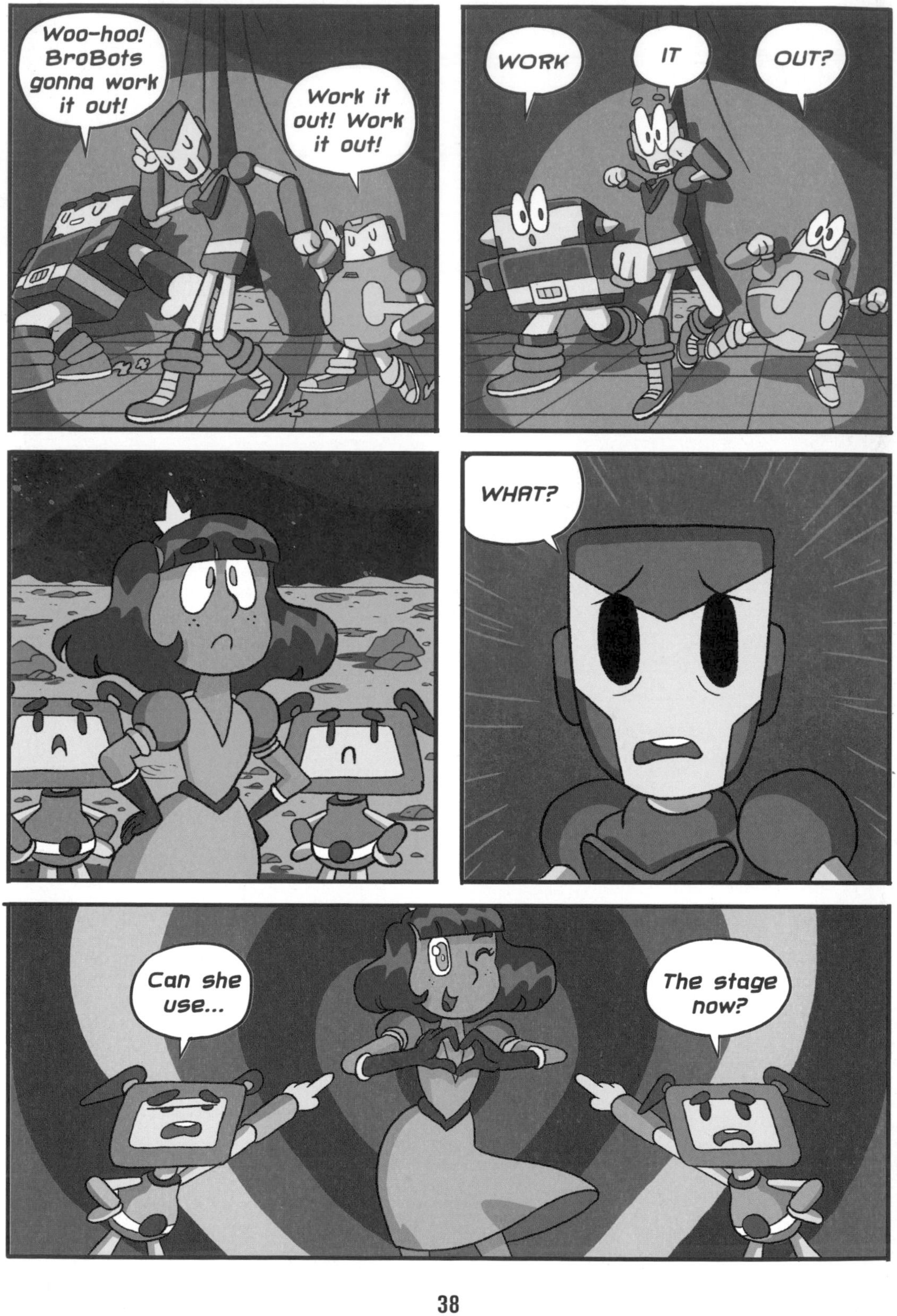
Woo-hoo! BroBots gonna work it out!
Work it out! Work it out!
WORK
IT
OUT?
WHAT?
Can she use...
The stage now?

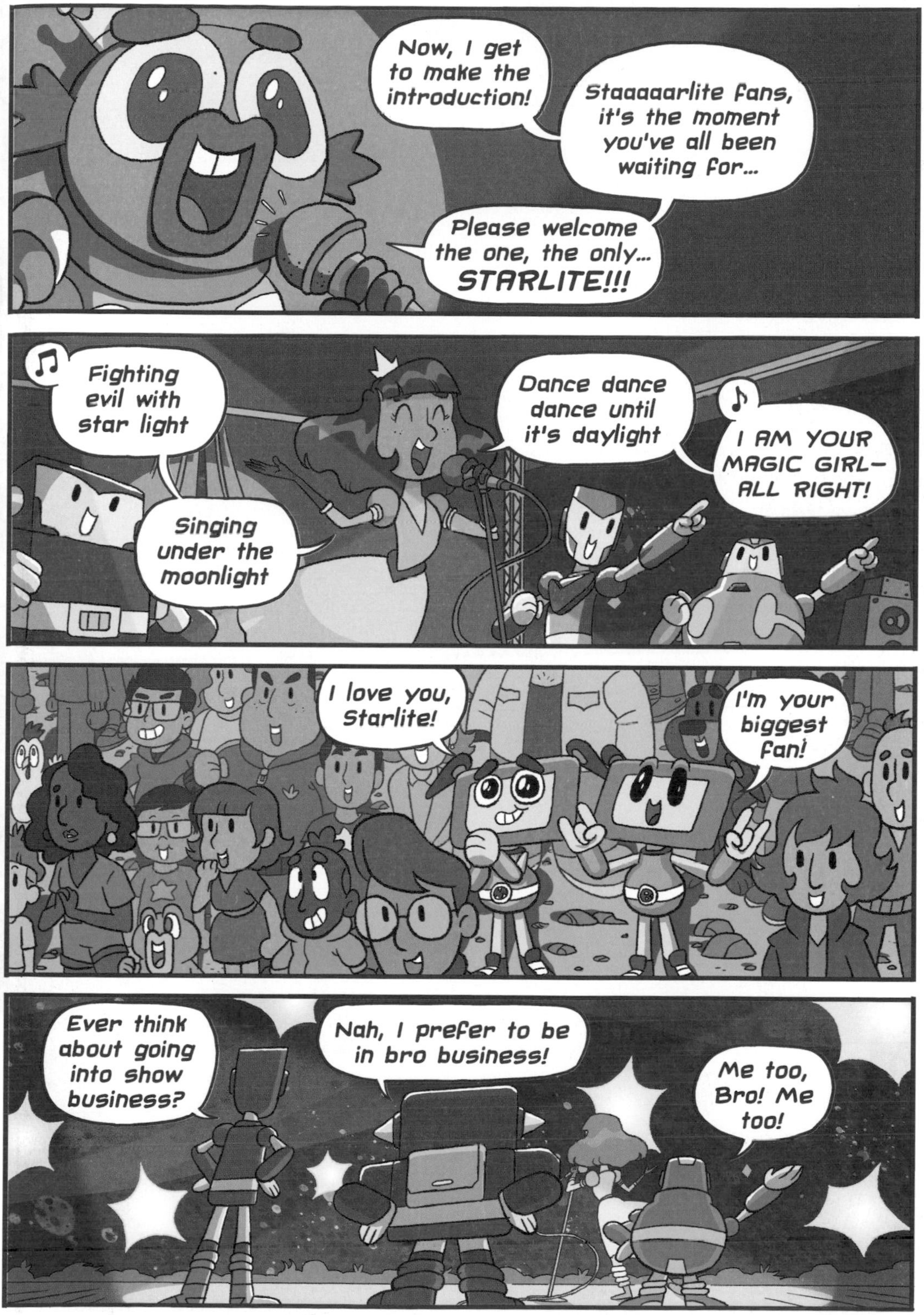

Now, I get to make the introduction!
Staaaaarlite fans, it's the moment you've all been waiting for...
Please welcome the one, the only... STARLITE!!!
Fighting evil with star light
Singing under the moonlight
Dance dance dance until it's daylight
I AM YOUR MAGIC GIRL— ALL RIGHT!
I love you, Starlite!
I'm your biggest fan!
Ever think about going into show business?
Nah, I prefer to be in bro business!
Me too, Bro! Me too!

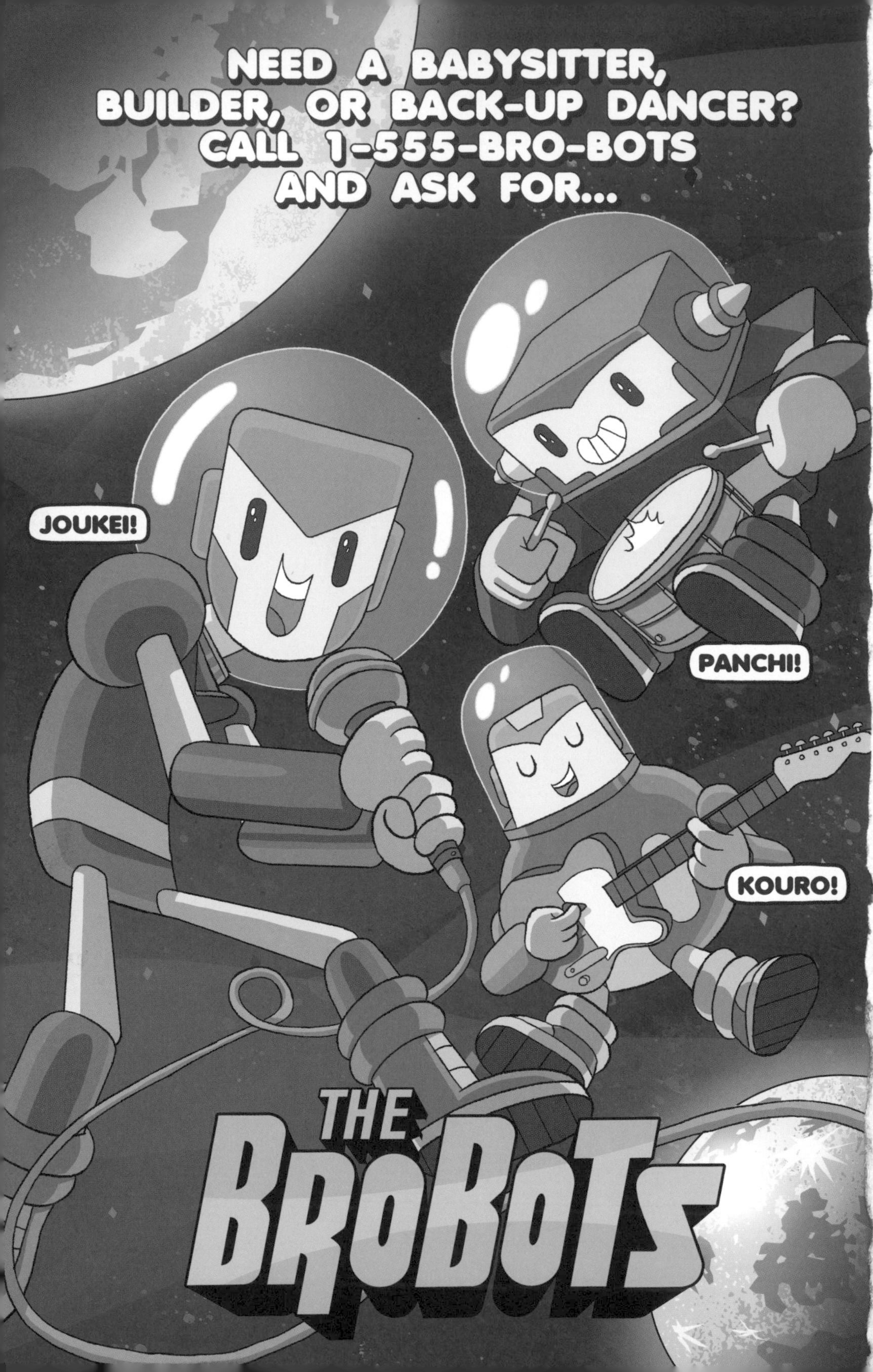
NEED A BABYSITTER, BUILDER, OR BACK-UP DANCER? CALL 1-555-BRO-BOTS AND ASK FOR...
JOUKEI!
PANCHI!
KOURO!
THE BROBOTS

About The Authors

J. TORRES

J. Torres is a comic book writer orbiting near Toronto, Ontario, Canada. His other writing credits include *Do-Gooders, How to Spot a Sasquatch, Rick and Morty Presents: The Vindicators, Teen Titans Go,* and *The Mighty Zodiac.*

His favourite princesses are Disney's Snow White, Mononoke, the Paperbag Princess, Starfire, and Wonder Woman.

J. would like to dedicate this book to his princess, his superhero, his sun, moon, and stars: his wife, Hye-Young.

SEAN DOVE

Sean lives and works in Chicago, IL where he runs his one-man design and illustration studio And Thank You For Flying. Sean self-published *The Last Days of Danger*, worked on *Madballs*, and draws his comic series *Fried Rice.*

His favorite princesses are Princess Bubblegum, Leia Organa, Nausicaä, Princess Zelda, and Princess Peach.

Sean would like to thank his parents, Rose, and 4 Star Studios.